PRAISE FOR

The HAUNTING *of* FALCON HOUSE

JUNIOR LIBRARY GUILD SELECTION 2016

NATIONAL PUBLIC RADIO'S BEST BOOKS OF 2016

CHICAGO PUBLIC LIBRARY
BEST OF THE BEST LIST 2016

GOLDEN KITE AWARD WINNER 2017

★ "[The] drawings, smudged and torn, provide eerie accompaniment to the text. . . . Middle graders unfamiliar with that history will be intrigued by the ghost story and the compelling setting, and explanatory notes both provide context and help to prepare them for such books as Candace Fleming's *The Family Romanov* (2014) and M.T. Anderson's *Symphony for the City of the Dead* (2015) later on. Eerie and effective."

—*Kirkus Reviews*, starred review

★ "The novel's fifty-six minichapters are interspersed with beguiling ink sketches of everything from star-soaked skies and stark graves to pitchforks and dozing kittens. The narrative itself—accompanied by useful footnotes for obscure phrases like *lorgnette* and *Corps des Pages*—is by turns wide-eyed, inquisitive, and earnest. This is a haunting at its very best."

—*Booklist*, starred review

"The creepiest middle grade ghost story of the year, so far. It's full of gothic horror in a huge and haunted Russian palace at the end of the nineteenth century, and it's a real page-turner, with a beautifully atmospheric sense of brooding darkness. . . . An excellent pick for readers drawn to the dark and gothic, who wouldn't mind spending time rattling around in a really spooky old house in the cold of a Russian winter long ago."

—Barnes & Noble Kids blog

"*The Haunting of Falcon House* is downright haunting. Author Eugene Yelchin has composed a mid-level novel that really takes the concepts of loss, grief, and our memories to a wholly different place. . . . [It] is a solid old-fashioned horror story." —KidsReads

"Yelchin sets his imaginative, layered mystery—prefaced by a tongue-in-cheek opening note on the story's purported origins—in late-nineteenth-century Saint Petersburg. . . . At Falcon House, events unroll with an odd mix of creepiness and comedy. . . . Offbeat, smudged sketches play a peculiar yet effective counterpoint to the evocative language, and helpful historical notes are included."   —*Publishers Weekly*

"In the introduction to this faux memoir, Yelchin describes finding the fictional prince's papers as a boy and later showing them to Laura Godwin (the real editor of this book) for publication. Set in late-nineteenth-century imperial Russia, the atmospheric story follows young Lev, 'the last of an ancient lineage,' as he arrives at the cavernous Falcon House in Saint Petersburg, eager to assume his noble duties. . . . Short chapters, an eerie setting, and a surprising twist at the end make this a compelling read for fans of historical fiction and ghost stories."   —*The Horn Book*

"Readers will enjoy the budding friendship, and the ghost story/ mystery is compelling. Absolutely nothing is overlooked—from plot similarities in the author's introduction to the haunting illustrations, which appear to be drawn by the protagonist. . . . A unique historical mystery from a celebrated children's writer and illustrator; a great option for classroom discussion and a jumping-off point for further exploration of Russian history."

—*School Library Journal*

"[Yelchin] very successfully merges historical Russia with a dark ghost story. Based on the premise of having found old notes and drawings from Lvov, the book is immediately mysterious and filled with wonder. There is the amazing setting of the huge mansion, filled with things like death masks and a basement of mothballed clothes. . . . Entirely gorgeous, haunting and deep, this novel is chillingly dark and wonderfully dangerous."

—Waking Brain Cells

"Readers who follow the axiom 'Nobody reads intros or endnotes' will settle right in for a great, creepy story, sigh with relief as Falcon House's real demon is purged, and close the books with a contented smile. However, those who follow the total immersion route—from the faux title page, to Yelchin's introductory remarks on the document he discovered as a child in Russia, to the notes that play it close to straight, commenting on relevant bits of Russian history—will appreciate the bonus delight of clever craftmanship. Additionally, those already familiar with Yelchin's work will discern the implicit indictment of an imperialist system entrenched far too long and unwilling to go out graciously."

—*The Bulletin*

The HAUNTING of FALCON HOUSE

The HAUNTING of FALCON HOUSE

Written by

Prince Lev Lvov

with pictures drawn in his own hand

Translated from Russian by

EUGENE YELCHIN

SQUARE
FISH

HENRY HOLT AND COMPANY
NEW YORK

**SQUARE
FISH**

An imprint of Macmillan Publishing Group, LLC
175 Fifth Avenue
New York, NY 10010
mackids.com

Our books may be purchased in bulk for promotional, educational, or business use. Please
contact your local bookseller or the Macmillan Corporate and Premium Sales Department
at (800) 221-7945 ext. 5442 or by e-mail at MacmillanSpecialMarkets@macmillan.com.

Library of Congress Cataloging-in-Publication Data is available upon request.

ISBN 978-1-250-11508-9 (paperback)
ISBN 978-1-62779-660-6 (ebook)

Originally published in the United States by Henry Holt and Company
First Square Fish Edition: 2017
Book designed by April Ward
Square Fish logo designed by Filomena Tuosto

1 3 5 7 9 10 8 6 4 2

To my mother

NOTE ON THE TRANSLATION

Many years ago, when I was a schoolboy in Saint Petersburg, Russia, my classmates and I were routinely sent out to collect paper waste. We went from door to door and pestered grown-ups to hand over old newspapers, magazines, letters, packages—anything made of paper that could be recycled. Afterward in our schoolyard, we sorted through the collected pulp before it was weighed and carted away.

On one such day, I came upon a bundle of paper held together with frayed twine. As I snapped the twine, decayed pages scattered. Some disintegrated at my touch, but others—densely illustrated with peculiar drawings, described in antiquated cursive writing—held. I hid the pages in my schoolbag instead of tossing them into a pile of paper waste. To my young mind, those pages contained an ancient mystery. I brought the pages home and attempted to decipher them, but they were out of order; the scribbled corrections, insertions, and crossed-out passages deterred me and, I confess, spooked me a little, too. I stuck the unread pages into the drawer of my writing desk and for the next few years ignored them, busy with other things. Yet those mold-crusted pages never lost their hold on my imagination, and when I finally left Russia, I brought them along with me to the United States.

Some years passed before I had a chance to share a few of those drawings with Laura Godwin, a publisher at Henry Holt. She admitted getting a shiver down her spine and encouraged me to translate the written pages. The task required infinite patience, but my initial impulse had been correct; the events documented in those pages did contain a mystery, one that a young Russian nobleman, Prince Lev Lvov, the author of the narrative, was attempting to solve.

Resolved to faithfully restore Lvov's original narration, I set to work. However, considering the poor physical condition of the pages, I also had to solve a mystery or two. There was no indication as to where the text began or where it ended. Many pages were missing or wholly illegible. The drawings were even more elusive. Some matched the events described, while others didn't, and some (like a drawing of the prince's chamber) seemed to have reshaped themselves over time.

I managed to establish a chronological order of the events and then divided them into chapters, matched the drawings to the chapters, and discarded those I could not match.

To carry Prince Lev's feelings across to the reader, I became inwardly connected to the young prince to such a degree that at times I even felt his presence. On occasion, while working late at night in front of my computer, I was startled by someone's touch, but as I turned to look, no one was there. I can't be certain, but as I typed Prince Lev's inner thoughts, I felt cool fingers firmly guiding mine across the keys.

Eugene Yelchin
Los Angeles, Winter 2015

Нашъ котъ Пушокъ

Это моя половинка.

А это мамины

CHAPTER ONE

*In which a mysterious boy
appears in the window*

Mother often hummed while sketching. I never mentioned it, not wanting to embarrass her. Once after nightfall in our dining room, she hummed the whole time while we were sketching Woolly in my drawing album. On the table, our cat snoozed as always, his ears twitching. Mother sketched him from his tail, and I from his head, until our pens met over his tummy in the fold between the pages. The picture was complete, the lines unbroken, as if one person had sketched the cat.

"Don't simply follow the rules," Mother taught me. "Draw from your heart, Levushka."

Whenever Mother talked about matters of the heart, she called me Levushka, but my proper name is Prince Lev Lvov, as was the name of every Lvov who has ruled Falcon House. My ancestors fought in every war and served every emperor since the great Tsar Peter. I was the last of an ancient lineage,[1] so when the invitation arrived from Falcon House for me to take up my noble duties, I knew the time had come to cut my mother's apron strings.

The journey to Saint Petersburg was long. The days might have passed quickly had I company, but my aunt Olga Lvovna chose to book me a private train compart-ment for my journey to Falcon House. As children ran laughing up and down the aisle outside my door, I dutiful-ly occupied myself with sketching or tossing rumpled pa-per balls to an imagined playmate. Mostly I stared out the window framed in hoarfrost as the train puffed across fields shrouded in snow. Snowdrifts flickered along the tracks, but far away walls of firs stood in the mist like mourners at a funeral. When at night the window turned black, I was startled by the reflection of a face. But it wasn't mine; some other boy's small, waxen aspect gleamed back at me, eyes wide, brilliant, and imploring. I blinked. It was my face again in the glass.

"Loneliness can play tricks on you," Mother liked to say, and, for a moment, I wished she had taken the journey with me.

CHAPTER TWO

*In which Prince Lev arrives
in Saint Petersburg*

Saint Petersburg[2] was so cold that when the train drew close to the station, the windowpane beside me transformed into a sheet of icy lacework. I breathed a clear eyelet onto the ice and peered through it. For an instant, the golden domes and spires of the city sparkled in the far-off distance, but then the engine's hissing steam blocked out the view. The train pulled along a platform cloaked in glassy mist, a whistle blew, brakes squealed, iron buffers clashed together, and the train ground to a stop.

Кучеръ Климъ

My aunt Olga Lvovna, my father's older sister, had summoned me to Petersburg, but she had not come to meet me. She'd sent her coachman instead. A man with a fiery beard was waiting for me on the platform. He said his name was Klim. I had assumed he picked me out amongst the passengers because I was the only boy getting off the train without parents, but I was mistaken.

"Had I not my own self many years ago driven Master's casket to the burial," said he, gaping at me in amazement, "I would have sworn he'd never died."

"Who died?" I said, a little uneasy.

"Your Excellency's grandfather, a man not to be trifled with." Klim crossed himself. "Your Excellency looks just like him."

Mother had never told me that I resembled my famous grandfather, but so much the better. What a nice surprise!

Klim tossed my trunk upon his shoulder and guided me out of the station to where his sleigh was waiting. I climbed in eagerly. Klim tucked me under a bearskin, mounted his seat, and took up the reins.

"Step lively, sister!" he called to his chestnut mare. The mare snorted and stomped the snow first with one foot, then another, as if she were of two minds which leg to start with. Klim twisted in his seat and winked at me good-naturedly.

"She's only kidding, Your Excellency," he said. "When she gets going, the Devil himself can't stop her."

CHAPTER THREE

*In which Prince Lev echoes
his famous grandfather*

Klim's chestnut mare flew like the wind. We dashed along snow-coated streets that sparkled like sugar, crossed bridges arching over frozen canals, and passed palaces gleaming with gold. Shops with enormous windows flashed by like tinfoil. The gas lamps had just been lighted, and below the lamps flowed crowds of richly dressed people. Sleighs and carriages I'd never seen the likes of crisscrossed in all directions. The crisp and frosty air rang with crackling whips, ringing bells, and sleigh runners squeaking over the dazzling snow.

At first, snowflakes twirled in the air like feathers, but soon they fell so thick and large that the sky became dark. The gas lamps, the festive crowds, and the vehicles we passed along the way vanished into the rapidly gathering gloom, but Klim's chestnut mare kept at full gallop. At such furious haste, snow began stinging my face while wind was howling into my ears.

It was then that I fancied my mother's arms cradling me under the bearskin covers. "Do not be afraid, Levushka, dear heart," she whispered into my ear softly. "I'm here with you."

"What's wrong, Your Excellency?" I heard Klim's voice. "You're crying."

At the station, Klim had said that I looked like my grandfather, so when I reminded him that he was to deliver me to my aunt's, I tried to speak the way my grandfather might have spoken. "Be so kind, my dear man," I said in a

grown-up voice, "as to refrain from needless chatter and carry out my aunt's orders without delay."

Just then, the sleigh skirted something unseen in the dark, its runners grating over the icy road. At the turn, a gust of wind struck me full in the face. I ducked under the bearskin, but with a terrible howl, the wind tore the covers off me. The mare snorted, stopped abruptly, and reared on her hind legs. A violent jolt yanked me out of my seat. I smashed into Klim's back, bounced off, and when I scrambled up, the sleigh stood still.

CHAPTER FOUR

*In which Prince Lev hesitates at
the door of Falcon House*

Behind the wall of thickly falling snow, Klim turned to face me, and as he spoke, the tiny icicles sprouting from his mustache broke off and fell into his snow-plastered beard. "With God's help we're home, Your Excellency!" he said. "There's your Falcon House."[3]

I turned in the direction his whip was pointing. A looming mass of darkness rose from the mist. With not a single window lighted, my ancestral home glistened as if some fabled giant had carved it from an enormous block of ice. The house ran the length of an entire street, but how tall it was I couldn't tell; the upper floors simply melted into the leaden sky above.

Klim tugged on the reins. The mare neighed and shook her head but didn't budge, as if refusing to approach the house. When Klim raised his whip to strike her snow-covered rump, the mare craned her neck and looked at him. Klim halted and, grumbling, put his whip aside and climbed out of the sleigh. Plunging knee-deep in snow, he trudged toward the entrance. Two massive stone falcons that I had at first taken for snowdrifts flanked the door. Klim passed in between the stone birds and tried to lift the large brass knocker, but it was frozen to the surface of the door.

"Open up, Lukich!" he hollered, pounding both doors. "I brought the prince!"

One door cracked open, and the shards of ice encasing it fell over Klim. A face framed by a pair of bristly

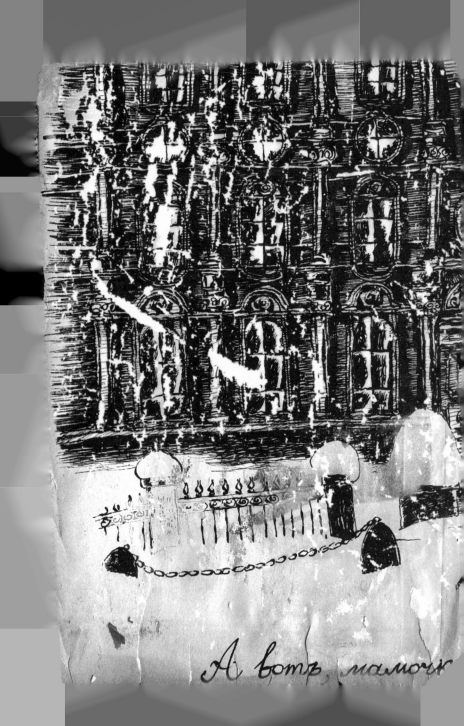

А вотъ, мамочк

Домъ.

Швейцаръ, Лужичъ сбиваетъ Клишу на...

whiskers appeared in the opening and looked severely at him.

"Fool!" cried the man. "What are you banging for?" Leaning forward, the man knocked Klim's hat off his head.

Klim winced and glanced in my direction with an embarrassed grin. The man followed his gaze.

"Your Excellency!" he bellowed, and, pushing Klim aside, rushed to help me out of the sleigh. "Thank God you're here. Madam has worried herself sick."

"What did you knock his hat off for?" I said.

"What hat?" He blinked, appearing not to understand.

I pushed his hand aside and jumped out of the sleigh.

"Name's Lukich," said he, following closely behind as I climbed the snow-covered steps. "Madam's doorman. This way, please."

I approached the doorway but halted before the threshold swept high with snow. One step over that threshold and my life would change forever. I would no longer remain who I was—a boy living with his mother, a boy with no duties and no purpose. One step and I would assume my proper place among my ancestors. One step and I would become the master of Falcon House.

"Be so good as to watch your step, Your Excellency," Lukich said. "It's slippery."

CHAPTER FIVE

In which a mysterious boy reappears

Falcon House's entry hall was vast and shadowy. An enormous chandelie'r loomed unlit above a staircase of gleaming stone. Along the walls in murky alcoves stood statues made of marble. The statues were of men in army uniforms adorned with crosses, stars, and medals, all intricately carved. Some men held swords in their hands, some held banners, some held rolled-up papers of great importance, but all seemed to be pointing their marble hands in my direction.

"Your ancestors, Your Excellency," Lukich whispered. "The Lvovs."

I turned to Lukich and saw myself reflected in a vast Venetian mirror suspended on the wall behind his back. Bundled up in scarves and plastered with snow, my puny shape seemed so pitiful compared to those grand marble men. I had come to Petersburg in order to follow the path of my ancestors, but gazing at my reflection now, I knew at once that my plan was doomed.

The front door stood wide open. Lukich had stomped off somewhere, and Klim was outside. If I was quick, I could slip out before they caught me. There was no time to ponder how to find the railway station in this blizzard or board a train back home without a ticket. I had to flee.

Turning toward the door, I was about to run out when a faint glow of something white atop the stairs caught my eye. The white spot hovered in the gloom for one brief moment, rose slightly, and suddenly swooped down along the handrail's curve. Halfway to the bottom landing, the white spot became a white shirt worn by a boy sliding

down the rail with lightning speed. When the boy's bare feet hit the floor, I glimpsed his face. It was the very face I had seen reflected in the train compartment's window, same eyes, wide, brilliant, and imploring. He glanced at me, smiled, and took off behind the stairs, vanishing as unexpectedly as he'd appeared.

The boy's remarkable appearance surprised me so much it was a moment before I recalled my intention of running away. I scurried to the door but on the threshold bumped into Klim hauling in my snow-covered trunk. I leaped back just in time; a lump of snow broke off the trunk and burst against the marble floor before me.

"Watch where you're going, fool!" Lukich shouted behind my back.

I glanced at Lukich in alarm, but he was not shouting at me.

"Do not be concerned, Your Excellency," he said. "I'll attend to him in short order." He glared angrily at Klim and tugged a bell rope hanging by the door. A bell rang out somewhere in the house. Another bell answered from a little farther off, and then a third one rang far away. At the top of the stairs, where a moment ago I'd seen the white shirt of that mysterious boy, a footman with a lighted candelabrum appeared and, leaning over the handrail, shouted, "Arrived?"

"Arrived!" Lukich shouted back.

"Thank heavens!"

Камердинеръ Шишка

CHAPTER SIX

*In which Prince Lev
allows an old valet to fall*

The double doors leading into the marble hall came open cautiously, revealing a throng of house servants. Whispering amongst themselves, they gaped at me with curiosity and fear. It seemed the servants were expecting some oddity from me, some rare trick, as if I were a circus bear. Lukich waved his fist, shooing them away, but they remained. Then someone bald and bandy-legged pushed through the crowd and hobbled toward me.

"Stay back, Shysh!" growled Lukich. "I am warning you!"

The old man ignored the warning and kept advancing. Lukich rushed to bar the intruder from me and swung his fist at him. The old man ducked under the doorman's fist, leaped forward, and caught my hand in his withered fingers.

"A living image of the master!" he whispered hoarsely. "God is my witness! You and your grandfather are as alike as two drops of water!"

I tried to free my hand, but the old man squeezed it tighter. "Allow me to serve Your Excellency, I beg you, or she will throw me out! I served your grandfather as his valet till he breathed his last. My name is—"

Suddenly he croaked and fell into my arms from a blow dealt from behind by Lukich.

"Name's Shysh," the old man wheezed, drooling from his toothless mouth. "At your service!"

Startled, I backed away. The old man fell.

"She's coming!" someone cried, and instantly the servants fled from the doorway. Shysh scrambled off the floor and hobbled after them, but by the time he reached the doors, they were already locked. He rattled the doorknob, scratched the door, and suddenly whined like a dog separated from his master.

There was a loud thud, a groan, and with a low rumble, something heavy began moving inside the marble wall. At first the crystals in the chandelier softly clinked, but as the rumble grew, they soon banged into one another wildly. The floor shook beneath my feet, and the Venetian mirror rattling in its frame made my reflection tremble as if in fear.

"What's going on?" I said to Klim.

He screwed his frightened eyes in the direction of the stairs and whispered, "Madam."

CHAPTER SEVEN

*In which Prince Lev is nearly
run over by a wheelchair*

There was a piercing screech, and something struck the floor behind the rumbling wall. The chandelier lurched, shedding crystals, which bounced off the stone floor like marbles.

"Attentio⁄o⁄o⁄o⁄on!" bellowed Lukich over my ear. "Princess Olga Lvovna Lvov!"

I moved away from him in case he'd bellow something else, but he fell silent and, with his chest thrust forward and arms pressed to his sides, gazed fixedly at the stairs. I followed his gaze, expecting someone to descend, but there was no one on the steps. Just as I glanced back at him, something banged near the stairs. I looked there again. A narrow door flew open to the left of the bottom landing, light moved behind the door, and someone in a tailcoat walked out backward. He towed a wheelchair after him, and when he swung the wheelchair round, I saw a pale-faced woman stiffen in the seat. Behind the door, a narrow cage framed with wrought-iron latticework swayed slightly within an ill-lighted room that had no ceiling. Could that be one of those lifting boxes Mother said they had in Petersburg? Called elevators?

Meanwhile, the wheelchair squeaked straight toward me so rapidly that I feared the man who pushed it aimed to run me over. Alarmed, I glanced at Klim standing to my left and then at Lukich to my right. They kept their bulging eyes fixed on the woman in the chair. As the wheelchair came to a halt before me,

Моя тётя княжна Львова

the woman raised a lorgnette[4] to her eyes and regarded me intently.

"God have mercy," she said under her breath. "Daddy's look-alike."

CHAPTER EIGHT

In which Prince Lev is questioned by his aunt

I had seen Olga Lvovna's pictures in my father's photographic album. In every picture, she smiled, her eyes shining brightly, and she was always dressed in white. That little girl was no more. Olga Lvovna was my father's older sister, but how much older I couldn't tell; she looked about a hundred. Her eyes were circled with dusky rings, her waxy cheeks were hollow, and all that remained of her once smiling lips was but a brief thin line. Her dress was black, and she was so pale and skinny, I fancied she had spent her life in prison with neither sunlight nor fresh air.

"Come give your aunt a kiss," said she.

I moved to kiss her on the cheek, but unexpectedly she thrust her bony hand under my nose. "You may kiss my hand."

I paused, a little surprised. Her narrow hand was richly jeweled. When I leaned in to touch it with my lips, the jewels flared icily. She flipped her hand palm-up and caught my chin between her thumb and forefinger.

"I must always be told the truth, Prince," she whispered, her black eyes piercing me like daggers. "The truth only. Do you understand?"

"I understand, Your Excellency."

She smiled faintly and released my chin. I skipped back.

"Then tell me about your mother, Prince."

I shrugged. What was there to tell? "She's fine," I said.

"Could you repeat that, Prince? I didn't quite follow. Did you say your mother is fine?"

I thought about it. "Not really."

She lifted her lorgnette and gazed fixedly at me. "Why not?"

"Because she didn't want me to come to Falcon House," I replied. "But she was wrong. She was dead wrong!"

I must have raised my voice a little. Perhaps I even shouted. The echo of my words was ringing through the hall. She gazed at me, astonished. My cheeks felt hot—I crimsoned.

"Mother was wrong to try to prevent me from my duties," I continued in my normal voice. "You called for me so I would become like them."

"Like whom?" said Olga Lvovna in alarm.

"Them!" I nodded at the marble statues in their shadowy alcoves. "I must become a hero and a general, like all the Lvovs before me."

She twisted round to take in the statues, and when she looked at me again, she was smiling. "The boy's ambitious," she said, as if I weren't there. "How precious."

For a moment, she scrutinized me through her lorgnette. "And how will you achieve that, may I ask?"

I stared at her, at a loss. I had never thought of that before.

"As expected," said Olga Lvovna brightly. "You don't know."

I shook my head.

"Do not despair, Prince," continued Olga Lvovna. "Since you are entrusted into my care, it is my duty to assist you. All you must do is follow the rules of Falcon House with precision, and in no time we'll make your wish come true. Woldemar?"

The man who had wheeled Olga Lvovna's chair stepped forward. He passed his hand over his thickly pomaded hair that shone like boot polish and said, "Yes, madam?"

"You are forgetting your duties, villain," said Olga Lvovna sternly. "A boy comes God knows from how far, and you don't even offer him a cup of tea."

Woldemar's expression became so frightened that I said quickly, "I'm not thirsty." Even though I was.

Woldemar gave me a grateful look.

Воладемаръ

"Well, if you are not thirsty . . . ," she eagerly agreed. "What are we waiting for? Is Prince's room ready, Woldemar?"

"As per your orders, madam, in the guest's wing we—"

She thumped him on the knee with her lorgnette. "Enough talking," she said sharply. "Move!"

Woldemar wheeled the chair round and swiftly rolled my aunt back toward the room where the wrought-iron cage was gleaming in the dark.

"Better catch up, Your Excellency," whispered Lukich. "She won't wait."

CHAPTER NINE

*In which Prince Lev learns the
first rule of Falcon House*

Woldemar backed the wheelchair into the cage, I squeezed in after him, and Lukich slammed the door behind us. I had never been inside an elevator and hadn't known how small they were. Olga Lvovna's chair took up all the room. My knees were pressed against the spokes of the wheel, and the sharp iron levers jutting out of the wall stabbed me in the back. Just over my head, a small gas lamp swung from the ceiling on a chain, but its dim light only made the wrought-iron latticed cage seem darker.

"Beg your pardon, Your Excellency," whispered Woldemar.

He leaned over me to do something to the levers behind my back. A bell rang out, the floor swayed under our feet, and the cage lurched upward. In fright, I grasped the latticework and glanced at my companions, but they didn't seem at all concerned. Perhaps that was the way elevators always moved. Embarrassed at my ignorance, I quickly looked away. Through the open latticework I could see the marble hall receding down below. Klim, with my trunk upon his shoulder, was marching up the staircase. Suddenly, the old man Shysh rushed Klim from behind and tried to seize the trunk. Just as they began to wrestle, the cage screeched up and I lost sight of their struggle.

"This is the first lifting machine of its kind in Saint Petersburg, Prince,"[5] said Olga Lvovna. "Your grandfather built it at great expense." She looked up at me through her lorgnette, smiling good-naturedly. "Daddy always tried to impress our dear emperor with all sorts of silly novelties."

Her smile vanished. "Until one of those novelties deprived Daddy of existence."

She waited for me to reply, but I couldn't think of anything to say. She lifted her eyebrows in disappointment and looked away.

The cage kept climbing up and the elevator shaft's decrepit walls kept crawling down. At intervals, gloomy stone landings drifted by. I began counting the floors but soon lost track. I turned to Olga Lvovna to ask her how tall the house was, but she appeared to be dozing, and I didn't dare to disturb her.

Just then, a sweet and peculiar odor reached my nostrils. I sneezed. Olga Lvovna's eyes popped open.

"What's that smell?" She sniffed. "Is that you, Woldemar?"

Woldemar's oily hair glistened, and pomade, melting in the cage's clammy air, was running down his cheek.

"It is simply unbearable," said Olga Lvovna. "I forbade you to smear that beastly stuff onto your hair, and you keep doing it." She looked at me. "The good that you do for your servants is always repaid with evil, Prince. They enjoy tormenting us."

I glanced at Woldemar again. He didn't look like someone who might enjoy tormenting anyone, but I could not tell for certain in the dimness of the cage.

"The first rule that you must learn, Prince," continued Olga Lvovna, "is to be strict with servants."

With a violent jolt, the cage screeched to a stop. A bell rang. The door opened, and Woldemar began to wheel the chair out.

"Take your hands off me, villain!" Olga Lvovna cried, and turned to me with a sorrowful smile. "Will you help an abandoned invalid, Prince?"

I looked at Woldemar. He gave me a little nod, and I understood that I must do what Olga Lvovna said. The handlebar was warm and sticky from the pomade with which he smeared his hair, but even so, I firmly grasped the bar and steered Olga Lvovna out of the cage.

CHAPTER TEN

*In which Falcon House gives
Prince Lev a shiver*

On the landing, a dozen servants holding lighted candelabrums had lined up to greet us. Klim, who had somehow reached the floor before us, was sitting on my trunk,
fumbling with his coat sleeve. The sleeve was so brutally
torn out of the coat's shoulder, I felt sorry to have missed
Klim wrestling the old valet Shysh on the stairs.

"Ah, the abominable coachman!" cried Olga Lvovna,
glaring at him. "One thing is missing from Prince's trunk,
and I will send you to Siberia in irons!"[6]

Klim sprung to his feet. Blinking rapidly, he puffed his chest out at attention, and his torn sleeve slumped off his arm.

"Imbecile," said Olga Lvovna in contempt. "You must learn another rule, Prince. Always be on guard with servants. They are all thieves and robbers."

How strange, I thought. If Klim was a thief and a robber, why did she trust him to bring me here from the station?

"Thieves and robbers," she repeated gravely, as if she read doubt written on my face, and turning away, she shouted, "Light the way, villains!"

The servants shoved at one another to take their positions, and in a moment, a ring of flaming candelabrums formed round us.

"Welcome to Falcon House, Prince," announced Olga Lvovna, "the home of the noblest family in Russia!" She gave me a quick anxious look and added hurriedly, "After His Majesty's family, of course."

I was beginning to be a little puzzled by Olga Lvovna's

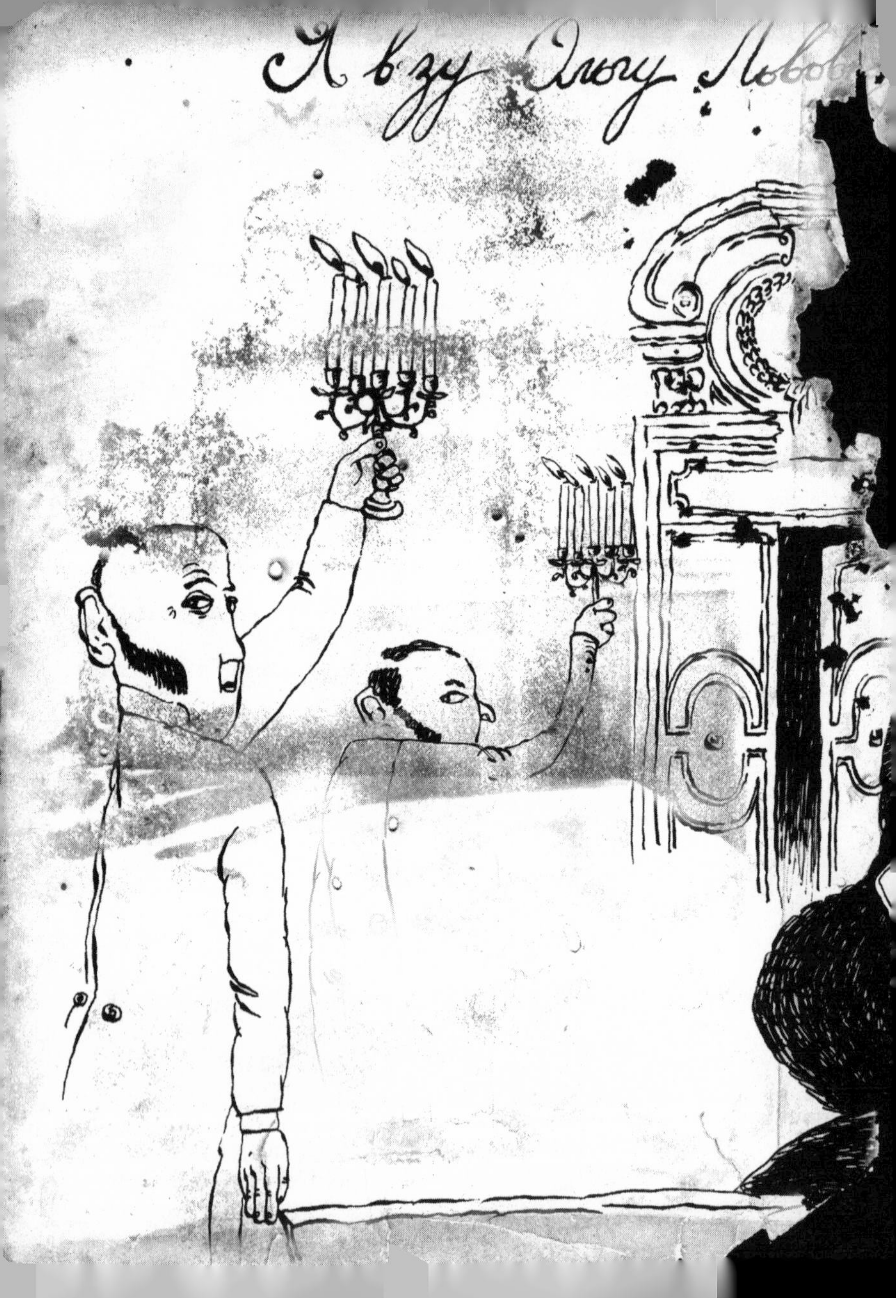
Я взу Ольгу Львов

stringent rules about the servants and was relieved that she had turned her attention to Falcon House instead. At home, I often fancied myself in the sacred rooms where my valiant ancestors had dwelled for generations. Now, when the moment had finally arrived, I expected to see something noble and lofty, but what I saw puzzled me even more.

The house was enormous. We passed through a succession of cavernous rooms, one after the other, cold and rigid and forlorn. The windows were tightly draped. Gray, dusty covers veiled the furnishings. The chandeliers were wrapped in faded cloth. Hung upon the walls, dim, blackened mirrors blurred our reflections, as if the mirrors had forgotten how to reflect. At every turn, the candles in the candelabrums flared and set monstrous shadows dancing across the walls. And then there was that smell. Stench, really, of something that had once lived and died but had not been buried. The smell was faint in certain rooms but pungent in others. As I gazed about, a chill ran through my veins. There was an icy draft traversing these rooms, but it was not the cold that made me shiver.

"I want to weep when I pass through these salons," declared Olga Lvovna. "Your father and I were so joyful here once, and so innocent. It is a pity that your father left us so early. He died when you were still an infant. And soon I too shall breathe my last, and this charming home will belong to you." She paused and added with a sigh, "And all that comes with it."

CHAPTER ELEVEN

*In which Prince Lev looks into
his grandfather's face*

The walls of the next dreary room we entered were hung with strange and dusty objects. At first I couldn't tell what those objects were, but as the candles lit them from below, I saw that they were human faces, or rather masks, and gruesome ones at that.

"What . . . what are these?"

"Your forefathers, Prince," said Olga Lvovna. "The death masks of the Lvovs. This was another of your grand-father's little hobbies," she added with an indulgent smile.

"The death masks of our ancient lineage."

"He made these masks?"

"God forbid!" exclaimed Olga Lvovna, shocked. "Born close to the sun, my dear, we are here to give orders, not to, you know, make things. Someone else made them."

"How?"

"No idea. First, I suppose, you need to die. Before they put you in a casket, they cast your face in something. Wax or plaster, I prefer not to know."

I peered about me uneasily. "Is my father here?"

She sighed. "You won't find your father's likeness in this house. Daddy did not allow it."

"Why not?"

"My poor brother couldn't be what Daddy expected him to be."

"And what was that?"

"What you wish to be, my dear. As true a Lvov as all those Lvovs who came before you." She flung a sideways glance at me. "Except your father. Rule him out."

"Why?"

Посмертные

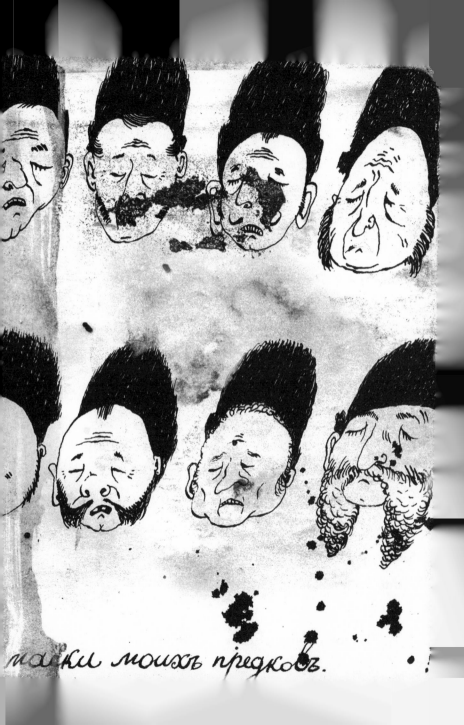

маски моихъ предковъ.

"He was too soft for that."

She looked away, as if to hide from me her changed expression, but I caught a glimpse of sadness in her eyes.

"Move away that light, fool!" she cried, perhaps angry that I might have noticed her momentary weakness. A servant with a candelabrum walking near her leaped away in fear. She cackled unpleasantly and swung back to face me. The sadness in her eyes was no more.

"Yes, Prince, unlike your father, Daddy was a real Lvov. A noble hero with a heart of gold." She gestured with her lorgnette to a mask on the wall. "That's him, incidentally. Hello there, Daddy."

Bewildered, I gazed at my grandfather's death mask. The leaping shadows cast upon his aspect by the moving light of candelabrums conferred upon it a peculiar impression of a living face. His cheeks were sunken, eyes tightly shut, and the drooped corners of his mouth seemed to gather into an unpleasant grimace; was Grandfather sneering at me?

"If your ambition, Prince, is to become a master of this

house," said Olga Lvovna, "you must consider him your role model." She glanced at me through her lorgnette. "After all, you look remarkably like him."

My heart sank as I peered at the mask. Did I look like that?

"Continue, Prince," she said. "Your chamber is just around the corner."

"Yes, Your Excellency," I replied, and eagerly pushed the wheelchair out of that dreadful room.

"Let us not stand on ceremony. Call me Aunt."

"Yes, Aunt."

"You are very sweet," she said with a pleasant smile. "I think we'll get along."

CHAPTER TWELVE

In which Olga Lvovna changes her mind

We entered a murky passage lined on one side with dark, worm-eaten doors. The passage seemed utterly abandoned, as if no living being had passed through those doors in ages.

"The guest wing," Olga Lvovna cheerfully announced. "This is where you will sleep."

At home, Mother's room was next to mine, and we kept the door between our rooms always open. Not that I was frightened of sleeping in one of these chambers by myself, but wouldn't it be better if I could share a room

with someone? That boy I'd seen sliding down the banister? Where did he sleep, I wondered.

"I have a question, Aunt," I said, pushing Olga Lvovna's
chair deeper into the passage.

"What is it, Prince?"

"Where are your children?"

She flung a chilly glance at me.

"I mean grandchildren." I hastened to correct my error.

"What grandchildren?" she answered sharply. "I am
still a maiden."

"Oh, I'm sorry."

"Do not be sorry. I had no shortage of suitors, my dear,
but your grandfather held them unworthy of our noble
name. No one whose family tree is younger than ours was
allowed to enter Falcon House." She grinned unpleasantly.
"Why do you think your mother was never invited to
visit?"

I peered at her for a moment. So that was why Mother
never told me that I resembled my grandfather. She'd
never seen him. And that was why she refused to take me

to Falcon House, no matter how much I begged her. She wasn't welcome here. Mother was not a noblewoman; my other grandfather was born a simple peasant.

"Why did you ask me about children, Prince?" said Olga Lvovna with a careless air. "You couldn't have seen any children here."

"I saw a boy who—" I bit my tongue.

"He was what?"

I hesitated. If Olga Lvovna had no children, the boy I saw must've been a servant. The first rule she wanted me to learn was to be strict with servants, so riding banisters would certainly get that boy in trouble.

"Oh, nothing," I said. "He was just walking."

"Just walking?" Olga Lvovna echoed. "Do you mean to say that you saw a boy walking in my house?"

I nodded. She startled me by giggling and clapping her hands as if she were a little girl. "Halt, fools!" she cried to the servants.

The servants walking on either side of us stopped abruptly, bumping into one another. I brought the wheelchair to a halt. Beside us was a door once richly carved but now grooved by worms into unfathomable patterns. My heart grew cold when I fancied what kind of room lurked behind it. Could Olga Lvovna really mean for me to spend a night alone in there?

"Woldemar!" cried Olga Lvovna. "Approach, villain!"

The servants parted, permitting Woldemar to pass.

"I have changed my mind. The prince will not sleep in here."

Relieved, I nearly blurted out *Thank you*, but I caught myself.

"Instead, the prince will sleep in his grandfather's study."

When Woldemar's face turned deathly pale and the servants exchanged frightened glances, all sense of relief abandoned me at once. Olga Lvovna thumped Woldemar's knee with her lorgnette. "Enough dawdling! Go fetch the key!"

Rubbing his knee, Woldemar limped away.

"I'm confident that you will find your grandfather's

study most stimulating, Prince," said Olga Lvovna. "Every master of Falcon House used it as his private chamber. Daddy spent his days there in contemplation and mental work, and if you want to be like him—"

"Yes, Aunt," I said, suspicious of what she had in store for me yet eager to sleep anywhere but in this dreadful wing. "I do want to be like him."

"Then you must rely on me, Prince," said Olga Lvovna merrily. "I will show you the way."

CHAPTER THIRTEEN

In which a door opens by itself

Grandfather's study was in the opposite wing of the house, so we had to march through all the cold and silent rooms again. While we marched, the candelabrums flared, the wheelchair squeaked, the nasty odors rose and fell, and when from time to time my aunt glanced at me through her lorgnette, I could not see her eyes behind the lenses that flickered with a feverish glimmer.

At last we reached an anteroom leading to my grand-father's study. I pushed the wheelchair toward a colossal double door opposite the entrance, but suddenly it grew so dark, I couldn't see beyond the back of Olga Lvovna's head, where a pale, waxy line parted her hair in the middle. When I halted, she spun round in her seat. "Cowards!" she shouted. "What are you standing there for?"

Instead of lighting our way as before, the servants with their candelabrums had clustered at the entrance to the anteroom, as if afraid to go any farther.

"Where's Woldemar?"

The servants made a path for Woldemar. He entered haltingly, paused at some distance from Olga Lvovna, and looked at her sideways.

"Did you bring the key?"

Woldemar produced a large key out of his pocket and held it up for us to see, as though a lifeless rat were hanging by its tail between his thumb and forefinger.

"Well, must I do everything myself?" said Olga Lvovna. "Unlock the door."

Woldemar passed his hand over his brilliant hair and looked at Olga Lvovna as if her request offended him.

"Enough of that," said Olga Lvovna sharply. "Do your duty." Turning to the servants in the doorway, she shouted, "Give him light!"

Exchanging whispers, the servants crept up toward Woldemar, and together they reached the door. Bent over the lock, Woldemar began fumbling with the key. Perhaps the lock was rusty, or his hands unsteady, but in spite of several attempts, he couldn't turn the key.

"Make haste!" snapped Olga Lvovna. "What is wrong with you?"

He grasped the key with both hands and tried to force the turn. He crimsoned from exertion, but the key refused to budge. He flung a fearful glance at Olga Lvovna and released the key. Stepping backward, he revolved his wrists and flexed his fingers, making ready for another effort.

Just then, the door creaked on its hinges and, with a long and mournful groan, opened by itself.

The candles flared in the sudden draft. Woldemar's shadow leaped across the ceiling as if fleeing from what lay

Вдругъ дверь открылась

behind the door, but the man himself stood rooted to the spot. In silence he gazed into the opening, then slowly turned his head and looked at us. His face was white as death. His mouth twitched, his eyes rolled in their sockets, and when he fell, his head banged against the stone floor. Somewhere in the house, a clock struck midnight.

Olga Lvovna yawned. "No wonder I am exhausted. It's past my bedtime."

CHAPTER FOURTEEN

*In which Prince Lev enters
his grandfather's study*

As if nothing out of the ordinary had just passed before our eyes, Olga Lvovna began giving orders to her servants. At first they were too frightened to obey, but she flew into such passion that her wishes were soon carried out. While the servants darted to and fro, not daring to spend an extra moment inside the chamber, Olga Lvovna and I remained in the anteroom, observing them. In no time the fireplace was lighted, the bed made, my trunk unpacked, and the chamber ready to receive me.

"Well, Prince, good night," said Olga Lvovna. "Be so good as to come and see me in the morning. We get up early here—duty before everything."

While she was speaking, I watched two servants dragging Woldemar's senseless body out of the anteroom. Poor Woldemar hung in their arms, his shiny hair slicking the stone floor like a mop.

"What's the matter, Prince?" Olga Lvovna frowned at me through her lorgnette. "You are as white as a ghost!"

"White? Am I?" I said, affecting surprise.

"If you are concerned about Woldemar," she said, following the servants with her narrowed eyes, "he's liable to fainting fits."

"What are those?"

"He passes out, Prince, from that filth he rubs into his hair. But on my honor, I'll put an end to it."

"Actually, it's the door that bothers me a little."

"Why should it bother you? It's a door, like any other."

"But it opened by itself."

"A gust of air, Prince, nothing more. It's a drafty house."

Вольдемаръ и слуги

"But why were they afraid to go in?"

"Who? The servants?" Olga Lvovna smirked. "They are fools, Prince. Fools. Take no notice of them."

She beckoned me with her shriveled finger, and after I leaned in close, she whispered, "I ordered the chamber to be sealed after Daddy's untimely departure. Nothing has been touched within, so the fools believe the room is haunted." She laughed and was about to turn away but then, as if recollecting a thought that had nearly escaped her, added, "You don't believe in ghosts, Prince, do you?"

"No," said I without much conviction.

She nodded in approval. "As expected of a man of your breeding. No Lvov was ever given to superstitions." She peered at me again through her lorgnette. "You said you want to be a master of this house like your grandfather?"

"Yes, Aunt."

"So let us begin by lodging you in Daddy's study. It'll benefit you greatly as well as, God willing, all of us. If, however, you're afraid to pass a night in there, I can assure you that—"

"I'm not afraid."

She smiled, turned to the open door, and for a moment peered into the study. "I envy you," she said. "How much I would have loved to enter Daddy's chamber."

"Why can't you?"

"Daddy did not allow that," she said bitterly.

"But isn't he . . ."

"Dead? He is indeed, dead for many years, but who am I to break his rules?" She shrugged. "Go rest, dear boy. You need repose. After the misfortune that has befallen you, you have fully earned it."

I studied Olga Lvovna for a moment, wondering what misfortune she was referring to. If she meant that my misfortune was to have been separated from my mother, her concern was misplaced. Mother and I would not be apart for too long. Without knowing it, Olga Lvovna was helping me to turn that misfortune into a fortune. Until today I thought that Mother did not want us to come to Falcon House, but in truth, she was not allowed to come by my grandfather. After he died, Olga Lvovna had not dared to break his rules and continued to bar my mother's entry. But when I became the rightful master of this house, there'd be no one to prevent me from sending for Mother at once. No one. Not even Olga Lvovna.

I smiled, and bowed, and clicked my heels, and marched into the chamber with that funny tingle between my shoulders that comes of being looked at from behind.

"Sweet dreams," called out Olga Lvovna's voice, and then someone slammed the door behind me.

CHAPTER FIFTEEN

*In which a wonderful surprise
awaits Prince Lev*

After what I had just witnessed in the anteroom, I was a little nervous entering the chamber, but a wonderful surprise awaited me. In the warm glow of the fireplace, I saw before me a study of a noble gentleman with a passion for weaponry and hunting. On walls draped with Oriental carpets hung sabers, swords, and daggers, and there were pistols and rifles of every conceivable sort. Wild beasts' mounts protruded from the walls; teeth, tusks, and antlers poked from everywhere. I wondered if Grandfather had

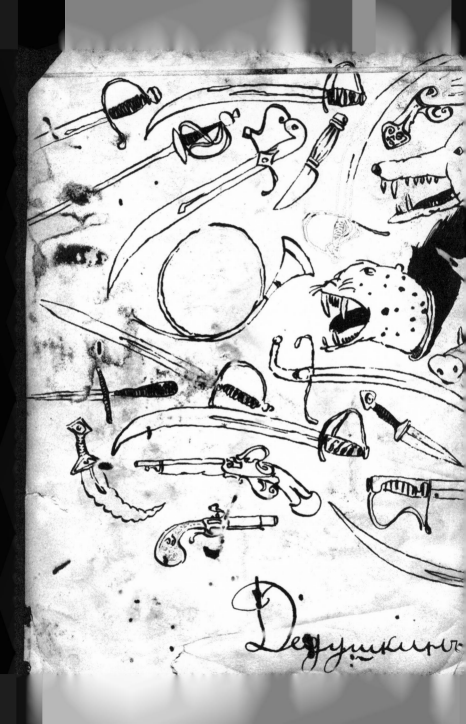

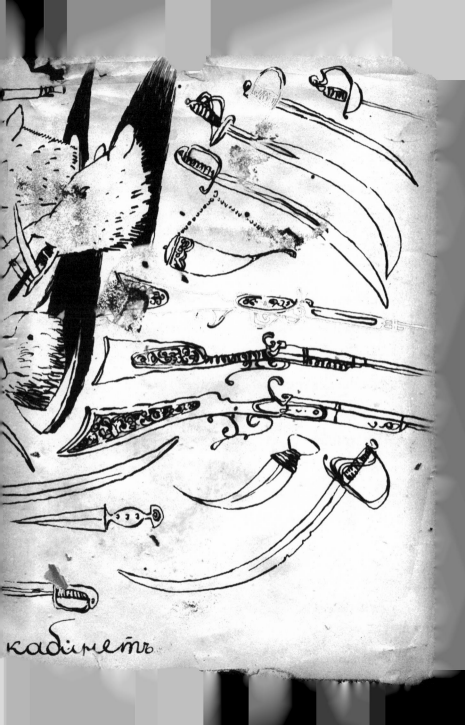

кабінетъ.

shot the beasts himself. As an army man, he did not bother much with comfort. There was a horsehair sofa on which a bed had been made, a desk of carved mahogany, a few mismatched armchairs—one made entirely of antlers— and a cabinet inlaid with pearl and full of books arranged in picturesque disorder.

I'd only seen such rooms in etchings made long ago. Back then, noble families had owned servants like one might own a dog, for example, or a horse. The servants all came from peasants who had to work the land like slaves, though they were not called slaves but serfs.[7] In those times, a noble gentleman could buy, sell, or swap whole families of serfs and even separate children from their mothers if he pleased. I didn't know why that was so; I wasn't good at history. Mother told me that the Lvovs had owned thousands of serfs, until one day our emperor decided to give the serfs freedom. Naturally, that was only fair. But looking at Grandfather's study, I knew that the hard labor of many serfs must have made him so rich that he'd been free to buy anything he wanted for this room. That confused me. Treating someone like a slave was bad, I knew that, but was it so bad to have the things you have always wanted?

CHAPTER SIXTEEN

In which Prince Lev plays musketeers

Mother didn't have money to give me many things, but she had always given me plenty of books. My favorite was *The Three Musketeers*,[8] the best book I had ever read. I hadn't read it all, of course—the book was very thick— but all the parts where the musketeers fought their foes I had read at least ten times. You could tell where the fights were in the book by looking at the pictures. I copied all the fighting pictures into my drawing album. The musketeers fought with swords called *rapiers*, and I had drawn rapiers

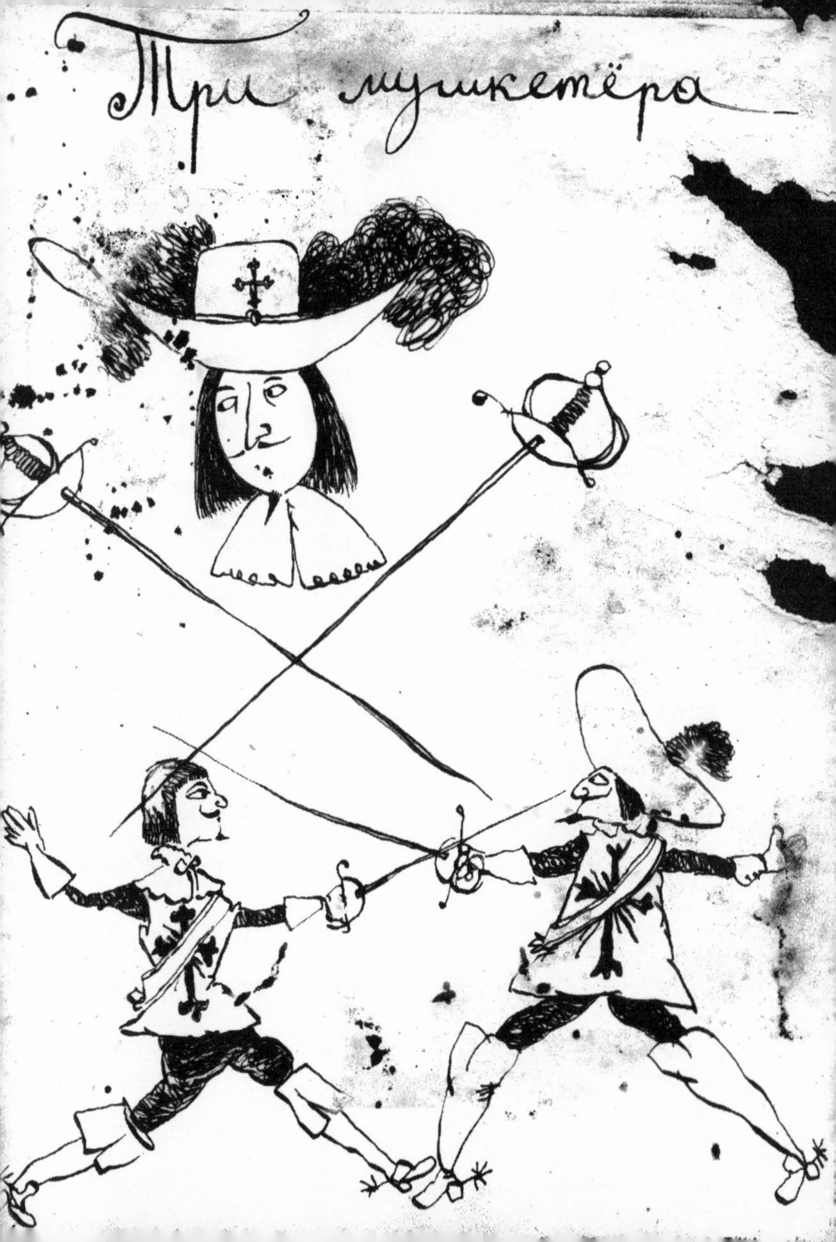
Три мушкетёра

over and over until I could render their straight blades without a ruler. I had never seen a rapier in real life—mine had been made of wood. But even if I had had a real one, with whom would I have fenced at home? Mother?

Eager to explore Grandfather's sword collection, I rushed into the chamber when my foot struck something on the floor. The object rattled away and bumped into the wall. I picked it up. It was a finely tooled rapier precisely like the ones I had drawn for the musketeers.

"En garde! Prêts? Allez!"[†] I said in French, taking on a fencing pose and slicing the air with my blade. I advanced, retreated, and advanced again. Oh, how I wished to have another boy to play with! I could have been a musketeer, and he could have been my foe, and we could have fenced until I won. Wouldn't that have been fun? That boy who had so smartly flown along the handrail down in the hall most likely was a decent fencer. Or if he wasn't, since he was a servant boy, I could have taught him. But how could

---

† *On Guard! Ready? Go!*—French.

I find him in this enormous and spooky house in the middle of the night? I wouldn't dream of trying. So I did what I had always done when I played alone—which was all the time—I put to work my fancy and made up my rival. He always looked like me a little, but I was the good and kind one and he was bad and cruel. I was a hero and he a villain, but sometimes, to spice things up, *I* was a villain. That was also fun.

I lunged at my imagined foe. He parried. Our blades rang out in the silence of the room. Sparks flew.

"You're a fine blade, monsieur!" I cried, advancing. "But I will slay you still!"

I attacked. He parried, counterattacked, and—Devil take him—pierced my arm. The wound was serious, but courage did not forsake me. I changed my sword hand and, fighting with my left, advanced, advanced, advanced. After one terrific blow, my opponent's sword flew out of his grip. He stumbled and fell. I placed my foot upon his breast, my sword point at his throat.

"Beg for mercy!"

Just then, I had a strong sensation that someone's eyes were watching me. Someone besides my imagined foe was in the room with me. I dropped my weapon. The rapier rattled across the floor. I looked up slowly.

CHAPTER SEVENTEEN

*In which Prince Lev is
frightened by an artist's trick*

Two piercing eyes were fixed upon me. I gasped and stumbled back. From the vibration of my near fall, the fire flared in the fireplace, light swept across the shadowy recess from where the eyes were glaring, and I saw their owner. A man hovered in the utter darkness. His body was distorted, strangely incomplete, swaying slightly in the flicker of the candles. I could scarcely breathe. A pale sheen fell across his features, and I became aware that I wasn't looking at the man but at his reflection in a dusty mirror. I spun round.

What I saw before me was neither a living man nor a ghostly apparition. It was a painted portrait of Grandfather. His face was brilliantly rendered. Each hair in his whis-kers and glorious mustache was outlined in lifelike fashion, but the eyes . . . the eyes! They positively stared. Small wonder that the servants were convinced this room was haunted. Grandfather looked alive, as if somehow he'd managed to escape the grave. His eyes fixed me with such a penetrating gaze, I felt uneasy. To escape his scrutiny I shifted slightly to my left. He followed me with his eyes! I shifted to the right. His eyes moved along with me. I nearly fainted.

But I didn't faint. Instead, I felt ashamed. How could I ever be like my grandfather when even his picture could give me such terrible fright? Besides, how could I fail to see the artist's trick? I knew that trick from Mother. Once, while we were drawing together, she'd sketched a pair of eyes with the eyeballs dead center in their sockets, so they

Дедушка

looked straight out. Then, regardless of how I moved in relation to her picture, those eyes stared back at me. I had always thought the eyes she drew were hers, and afterward, when I would stare at the picture, I had thought that it was Mother looking back at me.

In our cozy drawing room that trick had seemed so amusing, but in my dead grandfather's chamber in the middle of the night that same device frightened me to death. What I did next was truly shameful. I fetched a bedsheet from the sofa where my bed was made, climbed up an armchair, and hung the sheet over the portrait.

CHAPTER EIGHTEEN

In which Prince Lev calls for his mother

What I should have done was get under the blanket on the sofa, but I knew I wouldn't sleep. I didn't feel like playing musketeers anymore, so I looked round for something else to do. My gaze fell on my grandfather's writing desk. Olga Lvovna said that in this study Grandfather spent his days in contemplation and mental work. He must have sat behind this desk for hours on end, but that was years and years ago. Presently, a solid slab of dust lay upon the desk, and every object standing on it seemed to be shaped of dust as well—a crystal glass with dregs of some unknown fluid, a half-opened box of matches, and, in an ashtray, a cigar half smoked, resembling a cocoon. Beside the ashtray stood letter-writing implements: an inkwell, pens, an ink blotter, wax seals, and a stack of writing paper, all arranged in perfect order as if never touched.

At home, Mother, too, had those things, but they weren't so ordered. Mother was a little messy. She wore eyeglasses, and when we were drawing pictures, she'd always push them up her nose with her ink-smeared fingers, so after every finished sketch her nose would be black from ink. That always made me laugh.

I laughed. Ha-ha. In the utter silence of the room, my laughter startled me. Olga Lvovna said the study had been sealed since Grandfather passed away. Yet, in my fancy, the silence that had settled here was not the silence of a long-sealed room but of something more permanently enclosed, like a tomb. It was unbearable. I had to make some noise—to stomp my boots, to clap my hands, to shout something—anything to shatter that hopeless silence. Instead I whispered, "Mother?"—and waited for an answer, knowing that none would come.

CHAPTER NINETEEN

*In which Prince Lev sets out
to conquer his fear*

The top sheet of paper on Grandfather's desk was yellowed and shriveled, but all the others in the stack remained unsoiled. Cleaned of dust, the nib pen seemed very fine, with a grip of pearl. I dipped the pen into the crystal inkwell brimmed with sooty ink and recalled that I had read somewhere that in China they made ink by grinding bones charred in fire. The bones were probably not human, but still I tried to drive away the recollection—this chamber was not a place in which to think of bones—and yet such thoughts persisted to torment me.

In my mind, I saw a graveyard gone white with snow, dotted with crooked crosses and wreaths of rusted tin. In the silence, snowflakes were falling thickly against a marble tombstone. Before the tombstone gaped an open grave.

I shook my head to dispel the ghastly vision, and slowly it faded. I brought the pen to paper and at once felt someone's eyes watching me again. I looked up at Grandfather's portrait, but it was still covered with the bedsheet. I peered about me in alarm.

The light from the fireplace and the candles was enough to brighten only the middle section of the room, so the far corners stood shrouded in darkness. I didn't want to look in there, yet I forced myself. As I looked, I felt a strange sensation in my arm. My pen began to move across the paper. To my surprise, I saw that I was drawing the chamber. Somehow my hand knew before my head that that was exactly what I had to do. The very thing that frightened me must be conquered, and I would conquer it—if not by my grandfather's sword, then by his pen.

CHAPTER TWENTY

In which horrific events befall Prince Lev

My lines were bold and ink spatters flew, but capturing the likeness of the chamber was not an easy matter. The trembling light caused fantastic shadows to spring unceasingly from under every object. As a result, the furnishings, the weapons, and the mounted beasts kept shifting their contours. What was near appeared far and what was far appeared near. Before my eyes, the chamber took on startling shapes, as if refusing to let my pen create a faithful copy.

Time and again I wished to give up my drawing, and yet I couldn't. Some strange force drove me on, as if it wasn't my hand that moved the pen but the pen that moved my hand.

Increasingly the shadows grew thicker. First, inside the fireplace, a wisp of smoke spiraled upward into the blackness of the chimney—the fire had died out. By then, the candles placed round the room had burned below the brims of their candlesticks. Next, their flames flared, sputtered, and, one by one, went out. The chamber disappeared into darkness.

The last remaining candle flickered beside me on the desk. I kept still, not daring to disturb the flame, but suddenly it quivered and nearly went out. Startled, I saw that it was the swift movement of my hand across the page that had caused the flame to flare. I was still drawing the chamber! I tried to set the pen aside but I could not. My hand would not obey me! The pen kept sketching rapidly, rendering the chamber my eyes could no longer see. In panic, I gripped my right hand with my left and with all my strength yanked it off the drawing. My arms flung sideways and knocked the candlestick to the floor. The flame went out.

The darkness was complete. Terrified, I sat with eyes wide open, straining my ears to the gravelike silence. A dreadful moment passed. Suddenly . . . Oh, horror! Someone sighed so near me, a light breath grazed my cheek! I froze with neither voice to scream nor strength to move my limbs. Something stirred beside me, and a quick patter of bare feet hastened away in the dark.

I shot out of my chair, dashed in the opposite direction, and struck an object so sharp, it nearly pierced my chest. When I fell, scratching myself on its spikes, I knew it was the chair made of antlers. I lay on the floor, gasping, bathed in cold sweat, with blood pounding in my ears and my heart hammering in my throat, convinced that it was not I who had run into the chair but that ghastly chair had deliberately run into me. *Flee this cursed chamber*, a

voice screamed in my mind, *flee it at once!* Flee, but how?
What could induce me to look for the door in the dark?
In the dark, where some horrible thing was lying in wait,
ready to pounce and tear me apart!

If I could only rekindle the candle, I would have light—
not to see the monstrous thing but to locate the door and
run to safety. A vision of the half-opened box of matches
powdered with dust flashed through my mind. Yes, yes,
there was a box of matches on the desk. Come what may,
I had to find it.

Having no courage to rise off the floor, I crawled on all
fours in the direction of the desk. At intervals, I froze to
peer into the gloom and listen to the deadly silence. But
I heard nothing besides my violently throbbing heart and
saw nothing but the pitch-black void. How long it took—
hours or minutes—I could not tell, but at last I found the
desk. Rising to my knees, I groped about its surface.
Something shattered against the floor beside me—I must
have toppled the crystal glass. My fingers felt the ashtray.
At my touch, the cocoonlike cigar inside the ashtray

crumbled to dust. Then came the inkwell, the pen, and the sheet of paper with the sketch I hadn't been able to stop making. At last, the matchbox.

My hands trembled so much, I couldn't strike a match. The first match broke, and the second, but I succeeded with the third. The flame flared, the scent of sulfur hit my nostrils, the light cleaved the darkness, and . . . the match went out. I tossed it to the floor and stroked another. It burst into flame, crackled, sputtered, and continued burning. I found the candlestick on the floor and rekindled the candle. Lifting it above my head, I moved it side to side. Light darted up the wall, and in a brief flare between two moving shadows, I saw him.

CHAPTER TWENTY-ONE

In which Prince Lev meets Vanyousha

I couldn't explain it, but I was not at all surprised. Somehow I knew that before the night was out, I'd see the boy who had ridden the handrail down in the hall when I arrived. I didn't like to think about also having seen his face reflected in the window on the train, and so I didn't.

When our eyes met, the boy fell to his knees and cried, "Don't hurt me, spirit! Have mercy . . ." His voice quivered and he burst out crying. "Holy Mother of God, Father, Son, and Holy Ghost!" He clasped his hands and rolled his

white-lashed eyes. "Our help and our aid in distress, deliver me from this wicked spirit that besets me . . ."

The boy was so terribly frightened by me that my own fear vanished. "Stop hollering," I said. "I'm not a spirit."

He ceased praying aloud, but his trembling lips kept moving. "Not a spirit?" he whispered.

"Of course not. I'm a boy just like you. If you don't believe me, you can touch my hand."

I stretched my hand out to him and stepped forward. The boy shrieked, scrambled up, and darted behind the cabinet.

"Come out," I called. "Don't be afraid."

"I am afraid," came his little voice.

"Well, don't be. I won't hurt you."

The boy peeked out from behind the cabinet. "You must swear it."

"I don't need to swear. My word should be sufficient. I am Prince Lev Lvov."

The boy gaped at me for an instant, then fell to his knees and whacked his brow against the floor.

"Don't be silly," I said. "Get up."

He remained still. For a moment, I watched his sharp shoulder blades twitch under his soiled white shirt, and then I stepped to lift him off the floor. We nearly collided—suddenly he was on his feet. I leaped away.

"Hey!" I cried. "Keep your distance."

"Don't be angry, Your Honor."

"I'm not angry."

His doubtful, pale gray eyes seemed too large for his face.

"How did you get into my chamber?" I said.

He kept silent, watching me.

"You don't have to tell me—I know. You snuck in here before we came in and kicked the door from the inside to make it appear as if it had opened by itself. Am I right?"

He gave me a mischievous glance, and I knew that I was right. I smiled at him. "You scared everybody. What is your name?"

He shrugged, ruffling his flaxen hair. "Most folk call me names not fit to be retold in Your Honor's presence, but my mother . . ." He paused, gazed at me for an instant, and added softly, "My mother calls me Vanyousha."

"A boy your age should not be clinging to his mother."

"Why not, Your Honor? Don't you love your mother?"

"You mustn't question me. You are a servant and I am a nobleman. Don't you forget it."

He bent his head to one side and gazed into my eyes. "You love her," he said with satisfaction. "I can see it. I love mine too, Your Honor, and I miss her something awful. It's been so long since I was taken away from her."

"Taken away? Why?"

"Because I could draw pictures," he said, with such expression that I couldn't tell whether he was proud of the fact or sad. "No one else in our village could, but God chose to give me that gift. In the summer I drew with soot or with chalk; in the winter, with a twig in the snow. But if a scrap of paper came my way, God Almighty, that was a red-letter day, Your Honor, a real holiday."

A smile lit up his face, but only for an instant. His eyes dimmed as he continued. "When they brought me into town, they gave me real things to draw with and plenty of good paper. I was happy at first. They drove me in a fancy carriage from one palace to another to show off the gift God had given me. I drew pictures of my own choosing or whatever gentlefolk were pleased to look at. Once, they took me to the Tsar himself."

"Really?" I said in a mocking tone. "They took you to the emperor?"

"Saw him like I see Your Honor. God is my witness."

I smiled, not wanting to embarrass him.

"You don't believe me," he concluded sadly. "Only I'm not lying."

"You draw pictures for Olga Lvovna?" I said to change the subject.

The boy shook his head. "Can't draw anymore, Your Honor. God heard my prayer."

"What prayer?"

"I reasoned that if not for drawing pictures, I'd be at home with my mother, so I prayed to God to take back the gift He gave me. God heard me and took the gift away."

"But isn't that good?" I said. "Now you can go back to her."

He looked at me, wide-eyed. "But how can I go? My reasoning was wrong. I'm not free to go. My duty is to draw pictures, and if I don't, I'll never be allowed to see my dear mama. But I can't draw, Your Honor. My hands are clumsy now; nothing sticks to paper." His lower lip began to quiver, and his huge eyes welled up with tears. "What if you could never see your mother? Fancy that?"

I did not reply.

Vanyousha sniffled, rubbing knuckles into his eyes, but halted suddenly and, lowering his fists, peered at me intently.

"What?" I said.

"You are good at drawing, Your Honor. Your hand is steady."

"What of it?"

"Oh, Your Honor, Lord is merciful." He crossed himself. "He saw how much I suffer and sent *you* to deliver me."

"Me? What can I do?"

"Draw pictures in my place," he said, suddenly standing very close. "I beg Your Honor, draw for me! Help me to go back to Mother."

In confusion, I peered into his glittering eyes. Should I lend this boy a hand? After all, I loved drawing pictures. But what about Olga Lvovna? What would she think if she found out? She said that the good you do for your servants is always repaid with evil. But she also said that I must try to be like my grandfather, a noble hero with a heart of gold. If my grandfather had a heart of gold, wouldn't he be pleased to help this poor boy?

"I tell you what, Vanyousha. I might not be as good at drawing pictures as you are, but if you want me to, I'll try."

Vanyousha smiled, and his eyes lit up with such kindly light that it made his dirty, snub-nosed, and tear-stained face suddenly beautiful.

At that moment, three slow, loud knocks came from

the direction of the door. Startled, I looked around. I couldn't see the door in the dark, but I heard it open and bang against the wall. "Your Excellency's breakfast!" a hoarse voice called from the gloom.

When I turned back to Vanyousha, he was gone.

CHAPTER TWENTY-TWO

In which the old valet dances

"Owing to my experience in matters of etiquette," said the hoarse voice, drawing near, "I will serve as Your Excellency's valet."

The old man Shysh, whom I'd met at my arrival, was hobbling toward me with an enormous tray in his white-gloved hands. A single candle stood on the tray, lighting his gaunt face from below. In the surrounding blackness, his head seemed like a disembodied yellow skull floating in midair. When he approached, a putrid odor struck my

nostrils. The stench that spread throughout the house hung about the old man's whole figure. His tie, shirtfront, and gloves were remarkably dirty.

"I trust you had a restful night, Your Excellency."

"Is it morning already?"

"Early bright, Your Excellency. Your grandfather used to be awakened at this hour."

Unexpectedly, he thrust the tray into my hands and, with the frayed tails of his coat swaying, hobbled toward the draped window. Muttering to himself and moving with difficulty, he drew the drapes apart. Behind the double glass, the outer pane of which was snow plastered, the sliver of a yellow moon shone sickly against the pitch-black sky. Shysh called that early bright?

Meanwhile, the dust he shook out of the parted drapes was choking Shysh. He had a lengthy fit of sneezing that turned into a fit of gasping and then a fit of wheezing, but at last he recovered and hobbled back to take the tray from me.

"Did Olga Lvovna really send you?"

He seemed offended by my question. "Whom else would she send? Klim, the coachman—forgive the expression— sneaking in with your trunk when it's my duty to bear it? He's not worthy to serve a gentleman. None of them is. I'm the only one left." He peered at his tray and said after some hesitation, "I even cooked Your Excellency's break-fast. Can't trust the cook."

On a chipped plate upon his tray, a barely cooked slab of meat sat in a pool of blood. We stared at it for a moment.

"Is this my breakfast?"

"Your Excellency's grandfather was pleased to take in a rare steak at daybreak. 'Nature demands it,' he'd say."

"Did he?"

"He did, Your Excellency. A veritable lion Master was, a nobleman through and through, God rest his soul." He heaved a deep sigh, and his watery eyes looked past me into the room. "Expired in my arms in this very chamber, Your Excellency, right on that sofa over there." He nodded toward the sofa where the bed had been made for me. Good thing I hadn't tried to sleep in it.

Suddenly Shysh frowned. "Who did that?"

"Did what?"

He glanced at me severely, hobbled toward the covered portrait, and yanked the bedsheet off its frame. Satisfied, he gazed into Grandfather's face. After a moment, he shuffled slightly to his left, then to his right, then back to where he'd stood before.

"Master kept a sharp eye on us when he was living, and he does so from beyond," the old man said affectionately. "What eyes! Pure fire. One look from him, your heart would be in your boots." He glanced at me and added in a whisper, "He always kept a horsewhip at his side."

"A horsewhip? For riding a horse?"

Shysh peered at me for an instant. "To be sure, Your Excellency's grandfather was a fearless rider. He was everything a master should be." He wagged his head enthusiastically. "Yes, they were good old days. What fun we had! He liked to dress me in a bearskin and say, 'Dance for my entertainment, Shysh. Dance, you fool!' And I had to dance, Your Excellency, dance till I felt no legs under me." He twisted his mouth into a toothless grin. "Naturally, I was much younger then. In those days, I could really cut a dash."

Holding the tray before him, he shut his eyes and, swaying his bald, shrunken head side to side, began to stamp and scrape his feet, turning round and round, twitching his shoulder and flexing his bandy legs with effort. He knew how to dance well, but he had no strength now. Soon his face became ashy and spit dribbled from his toothless mouth. He broke off with a sob, stumbled, and his tray clashed to the floor.

This time I didn't let him fall. I caught the old man and tried to help him to an armchair, but he drew away, ashamed to look at me. I collected his tray off the floor and handed it back to him.

"It's not true that Olga Lvovna sent you to be my valet, is it?"

Shysh chewed his lips but did not reply.

"Why did you lie to me?"

He sighed. "Madam wants to put me out, Your Excellency," he said. "But where would I go? All I can do is serve the masters. If she finds out that I have troubled you . . ." He broke off and glanced at me from under his wiry eyebrows. "I beg Your Excellency, don't tell her that I came in here."

I was certain that Olga Lvovna had a rule by which you were forbidden to believe the servants. I felt sorry for the old man but had to follow the rules.

"I won't tell her," I said sternly, "but never lie to me again and do not come here, do you understand?"

Shysh lurched to kiss my hand, but I snatched it away from him. He bowed slowly and deeply and shuffled out of the room. I watched him until he disappeared in the darkness, then heard the door close softly after him.

CHAPTER TWENTY-THREE

*In which Prince Lev sets out to write
a letter but draws pictures instead*

Blame it on my strange aunt and her spooky house, or blame it on the boy pitiful enough to eat a hole in your heart and that old valet dancing on his spindly legs, but by the time a gray morning light seeped into the chamber, I really missed my mother. I had always wanted to write her a letter, but we had never been apart until now. So, behind my grandfather's desk I sat, wishing to tell Mother all that had happened to me in just one night, but somehow instead of words, pictures came out.

I drew the train that had brought me to Petersburg, I drew Klim the coachman and his horse, and I drew Lukich, the rude doorman. I drew the fancy carriages that I had seen on the way to Falcon House, and I drew my aunt Olga Lvovna and Woldemar and Vanyousha and the old valet Shysh, and I drew what I saw in the house and in my grandfather's study. My hand kept drawing and drawing, tirelessly, as if it knew just what to draw before I even thought of it—and knew *how* to draw it too. But what was most surprising, my pictures were turning out really well.

That pleased me very much, for I wanted not only to impress Mother with my drawings but also to prove her wrong. Mother taught me not to follow the rules. "Draw from your heart," she said. What she meant by drawing from the heart was still far from clear, but I knew for certain now that she was wrong about not following the rules. To become a master of Falcon House, I was called to follow its rules with precision. Lodging in my grandfather's chamber, occupied before me by every master of this house, was surely one of those rules. And that was why the drawings I was making at my grandfather's desk were much better than the ones I used to make at home with Mother.

My last drawing was of Shysh, and as I wrote next to it, "This is Shysh bringing me my breakfast," there was a knock on the door. The sound was timid and brief, more like a scrape than a knock. I felt myself smiling. Vanyousha had slipped out last night, frightened by the old man coming, and I was certain that it was he at the door. I called out for him to come in, but the door remained closed. I went to the door and opened it, but he was not outside.

"Vanyousha?"

Someone coughed in the shadows. A figure detached itself from the wall, and the crown of a hairless head caught a glint in the pale, slanting light.

"Shysh!" I said angrily. "Didn't I tell you not to come here again?"

"It's Woldemar, Your Excellency," the figure replied. "Madam is asking for you."

Woldemar stepped into the light and, when he bowed,

Володемаръ съ бритой голов

I saw that his hair was shorn to the skin. He crimsoned and passed his hand over what last night had been a head full of beautiful hair but now shone smooth and pink.

"It's fresher this way, Your Excellency," he said. "Summer is coming."

It was a long time until summer, but when I saw how terribly embarrassed he was, I restrained myself from pointing that out.

While I put on my jacket and folded the drawings I had made for Mother into my pocket, Woldemar waited in the anteroom, standing far away from the door. He had fainted last night when the door came open, and now even the sight of it clearly made him uneasy.

On the way to Olga Lvovna's, I followed Woldemar through the same rooms we'd passed through before. The rooms stood as then, cold, rigid, and forlorn, but presently, winter light oozing through the gaps in the window drapes made them look pitiful, not scary. We went up in the creaky elevator, then walked through a long and gloomy

Князь

Левъ Львовичъ
Львовъ

рождёнъ в 1879 году
умеръ в...

passage with peeling stucco, and at last reached the recep‑
tion room before Olga Lvovna's private chamber.

In the bare room with floral wallpaper so faded, you
couldn't tell what kind of flowers were printed on it, my
aunt's wheelchair stood waiting for her by the door. Beside
the door, in a large frame once richly gilded, a painting of
the Lvov family tree hung on the wall. The nameplates
of my ancestors dangled off the branches of the tree like
Christmas decorations. Under each name, the dates of
birth and death were written. At the bottom of the trunk,
branches were thick and leafy, but at the top, the tree
thinned out to a lonely twig. My nameplate drooped
off that twig—PRINCE LEV LVOVICH LVOV, BORN 1879,
DIED—

CHAPTER TWENTY-FOUR

In which Prince Lev visits with his aunt

Olga Lvovna's chamber smelled of sickness. By the sofa upon which she reclined under a black shawl stood a side table crowded with medicine bottles, and below it, a low tub with something brownish floating inside.

"Come sit beside me, Prince," said Olga Lvovna feebly. "Bring Prince a chair, Woldemar."

He picked up a chair.

"Not that one!" she said, annoyed. "The one with a leather cushion."

He set down the chair and lifted another.

"Do not dawdle. Bring it here."

He tiptoed around the sofa and set the chair down.

"Closer."

He moved the chair.

"Closer still."

He did.

"Really, Woldemar! It is enough to try the patience of an angel. Bring it closer."

Just as he touched the chair to move it closer, she shrilled, "That's too close! Leave it there."

While Woldemar tiptoed into the corner, Olga Lvovna followed him with angry eyes, but as she turned to me, a pleasant smile played upon her thin, pale lips. "Be seated, Prince."

I sat.

"You do not look well." She peered at me through her lorgnette. "Had you any sleep?"

I opened my mouth to reply, but she broke in. "*I* had a sleepless night. Upset of nerves, convulsions, other symptoms too horrid to describe. The doctors fear for my life, did I tell you that?"

"No, Aunt."

"I did not want to worry you. It's dreadful. But enough about me. Talk, Prince, talk. We must have clever conversation."

A moment passed in silence.

"Anything you wish to tell me about sleeping in your grandfather's study?" she said with a careless air. "Was it sufficiently quiet? Any unusual noises? Sudden changes of temperature? Doors opening by themselves? Ghostly visions perhaps?" She cackled and her eyes flashed excitedly behind the lenses of her lorgnette.

I stared at her attentively for a moment.

"No, but . . ."

"But what?" She leaned in eagerly.

"Could you send something to my mother?"

She peered at me. "By all means," she said after a pause. "It will give me pleasure."

I pulled the stack of folded drawings from my pocket.

"For mercy's sake, Prince, no wonder you're worn out! Look at all these pages."

Without warning, she grasped the drawings. Startled, I clutched onto them, and when we pulled in opposite directions, the loose sheets burst from under our fingers, cascading to the floor.

"Woldemar!" she cried, but he was on his knees already, gathering the sheets.

"Now the pages are out of order," I said, a little upset.

"Rest easy, Prince. I will sort them out." Olga Lvovna snatched the pages from Woldemar and eagerly leafed through them. "You drew pictures! How delightful. Why, you have a real talent, Prince." Olga Lvovna smiled at me, turned over a sheet, and lost her smile. "And who is this, allow me to ask?"

My face turned very hot. She had come upon a portrait I made of her.

"I have always maintained," said Olga Lvovna after an

uncomfortable silence, "that in art as in life, honesty is the most important feature." She closed her eyes and added in a suffering tone, "Woldemar, take these away. I feel a little faint."

Woldemar took the drawings from Olga Lvovna. Her hand fell listlessly upon the shawl. "Did I take my laurel drops today?"

"Yes, madam. Twelve drops after your morning coffee, per doctor's orders."

"Give me more."

Woldemar set my drawings down on the side table among the medicine bottles and began pouring drops from a small vial into a glass of water, moving his lips as he counted the drops. When he turned to Olga Lvovna with the glass, her eyes were closed. She appeared to be dozing.

After several minutes had passed, I tugged Woldemar on the sleeve. "She's sleeping," I whispered. "Can't I go?"

He glanced at me in horror and pressed his finger to his lips. "Shh!"

Olga Lvovna's eyes popped open. She glared at Woldemar standing above her. "Aaaah!" she shrieked, and pulled the shawl over her head.

Surprised, I looked up at Woldemar. He shrugged.

"What are you hovering over me for, villain?" Olga Lvovna's muffled voice came from under the shawl. "You want to strangle me?"

"Your laurel drops, madam."

She yanked the shawl down, exposing her angry face. "What laurel drops? Go away."

Woldemar set the glass down on the side table and slinked into the corner.

Olga Lvovna looked at me in surprise. "Ah, Prince Lev," she said as if she were seeing me for the first time this morning. "So nice of you to drop by."

How odd she was. I glanced at Woldemar again, but he pretended that he didn't see me looking.

"But why don't you speak?" said Olga Lvovna. "Speak, Prince, speak. Let us choose a subject for a conversation. For example . . . do you like your chair?"

Дѣдушкинъ стиль

"What chair?"

"The chair you are sitting on."

I looked at it. "I don't know. Why?"

"It was Daddy's favorite. He used to sit in it when I danced for him." She narrowed her eyes at me. "You are not the only one with artistic talent, Prince, you know."

She had not at all forgotten looking at my drawings before she fell asleep. Or was she just pretending to be sleeping?

"You did not know that I used to dance? Indeed, how could you? By the looks of this pathetic invalid, who could tell that she was expected to become a ballet sensation? But"—she heaved a deep sigh—"your grandfather would not allow it."

"Why not?"

"He didn't like dancing, I suppose."

"If he didn't like dancing, why would he make Shysh dance until he—"

Olga Lvovna's lorgnette flashed up to her eyes. "What?"

I bit my tongue. I had given the old man my word that I wouldn't tell her. What was I thinking, blabbering like that?

"How would you know that?" Olga Lvovna frowned and glanced at Woldemar. He turned pale.

"Did he dare come to your chamber?" she inquired. When I didn't reply, Olga Lvovna continued. "I'm deeply grieved, Prince, that you let yourself be deceived by a liar. Shysh no sooner opens his mouth than out comes a lie. Isn't that so, Woldemar?"

Woldemar cleared his throat but made no reply.

"Speak up!"

"Yes, madam."

"*Yes, madam,*" Olga Lvovna said, mocking his voice. "What is that liar still doing in my house, allow me to ask?"

"I told him—"

"Hold your tongue!" she shouted. "You told him . . . Your duty is to obey orders and not to talk!" She turned to me and said, trying to conceal fury in her voice, "Another rule of this house, Prince, is never to believe what servants tell you. They are given to lying." Her flaming eyes darted to Woldemar. "Am I right, Woldemar?"

Woldemar peered at the floor.

"Come, look me in the face, villain! I had your hair chopped off. Next I'll chop your head off!"

Woldemar flung me an imploring glance.

"Look at me, not at him!" Olga Lvovna snatched the glass with her laurel drops and hurled it at Woldemar. He ducked and the glass burst against the wall.

I didn't know how it happened that I was no longer sitting in Grandfather's favorite chair but standing instead between Olga Lvovna and Woldemar, as if shielding him from her wrath.

"Why—why do you treat them like slaves? The Tsar gave them freedom."

She gazed at me for a moment, patted around for her lorgnette, found it, and, peering through it, said with a mocking smile, "I beg you to forgive me, Prince. Like all invalids, I'm a little irritable on occasion. I assure you that at other times I treat my servants as if they were my own children."

I fancied for an instant how she might have treated her children had she had any, but after a glance at Woldemar's shorn head, I drove that fancy far, far away.

"I couldn't find an envelope to put my drawings in," I said. "Please remember to send them to my mother."

"I won't forget it, Prince. Regrettably, my memory is sound."

CHAPTER TWENTY-FIVE

*In which Prince Lev learns
what was in store for Shysh*

Riding the elevator back to my chamber, I felt Woldemar's sidelong glances and guessed that he wanted to tell me something but did not dare.

"My aunt is hard on you," I said to break the silence.

"I don't complain, Your Excellency," he eagerly replied. "I don't get punished for nothing."

"She had your head shaved, Woldemar. That's terrible."

"With God's help, it'll grow back, Your Excellency. And summer's coming."

"Summer is not coming for a long time. You don't have to pretend with me, you know? She mistreats you."

He glanced at me but didn't reply, and for several minutes we rode in silence. Then after a lengthy hesitation, he looked at me and said, "To be sure, Madam can roast you to the quick if she's in the mood for it, but deep inside, she's a sorry woman."

"What do you mean, sorry?"

"It's not for us serving people to judge our benefactors, Your Excellency," he said carefully, "but your grandfather, God rest his soul, was mighty strict with her." Then his face brightened. "But Your Excellency will be different. You will make a fair master."

"Why is that?"

"In all my service, I've never seen a soul stand up to Madam for the way she rules us," he said. "I wish I were that brave."

Brave? He should have seen me losing my wits last night after Vanyousha spooked me in the dark. "I'm not brave, Woldemar."

"Oh, very brave indeed. No one ever slept the night in the haunted room before Your Excellency."

The elevator cage let out a piercing screech, shuddered, and halted between the landings. Woldemar paled and crossed himself.

"Nonsense, Woldemar. The room is not haunted."

"Not haunted?"

"Of course not. It's only a silly superstition."

The cage rattled in place for a moment, then lurched suddenly and started moving again.

By the look on Woldemar's face, I knew he did not believe me.

"Why was my aunt so angry with you about Shysh?" I said, to change the subject.

"Shysh?" He shook his head, grinning. "The old dog doesn't know how to stay out of trouble, Your Excellency."

"What trouble?"

"Judge for yourself, Your Excellency. Madam ordered me to turn him out of the house on account of uselessness. She said it's wicked to eat bread without working for it. Madam's right, but how could I turn him out? He'd freeze to death. It's wintertime. So I hid him down in the mothballs. Stay as quiet as a mouse, I said, out of sight, out of mind. I was right; Madam clean forgot about him. But then Your Excellency arrived, and the old dog is back to his tricks. He bothered you last night, as you were pleased to mention to Madam. Now she will drive him out for certain. She doesn't like half measures."

So if that old man froze to death, I'd be the one to blame. I hadn't meant to, but I failed to keep my noble word. What kind of a master would I be to them?

"What do you mean, you hid him in the mothballs?"

"The mothballs, Your Excellency? Why, they're

down in the cellar. They keep your family's garments down there going back to olden times. Such peculiar costumes . . ." He chuckled and shook his head but instantly turned serious again. "It's best Your Excellency keep away from the cellar. Madam won't like it."

CHAPTER TWENTY-SIX

In which Woldemar attempts to be brave

The cage screeched to a halt, and a young, red-haired footman swung the door open. "Good morning, Your Excellency!" he cried, gaping at me. "Have a good night's sleep, Your Excellency? Nothing to disturb Your Excellency?"

On the landing behind the footman, three other servants stretched their necks to get a better look at me. To them I was someone who had spent a night in a haunted chamber and lived to tell the truth. But what truth was there to tell? My eerie intruders turned out to be a sad old man and an even sadder boy.

"Quit yapping," Woldemar snapped at the red-haired footman. "Run to the kitchen and tell the cook His Excellency will be needing a bite to eat. He'll know what to do. Run like the wind, you hear?"

The footman blinked, spun round, and ran off so fast, the three servants had to leap out of his way.

How they managed it I could not even fancy, but by the time Woldemar and I reached Grandfather's chamber, a tray of food was waiting for us by the door. Shysh had brought the raw slab of meat on that same tray, but now a mouthwatering spread was laid out on it: pies and pancakes and a small samovar, puffing steam.

Knowing how frightened Woldemar was of my chamber, I took hold of the tray to take it in myself, but he snatched it away.

"God forbid, Your Excellency! What if Madam finds out that I let you do my duties?"

I shrugged and, whistling a careless tune, strolled

through the door to show him that there was nothing to be scared of inside. When I reached the writing desk, I turned round and saw Woldemar still at the threshold, unable to cross it.

"Remember, Woldemar," I called out, "it's only a superstition."

He stretched his lips in a failed attempt at a smile and, after a painful hesitation, stepped into the chamber.

I watched him creep along, knees bent, hands shaking, screwing his eyes, now over one shoulder, now over the other, as if expecting someone to leap at him from behind, and when at long last he reached the desk and set the tray with rattling cups and plates upon it, his face was red and soaked in perspiration.

"Bravo, Woldemar!" I clapped my hands. "That was very brave!"

He groaned in relief, pulled a handkerchief out of his pocket, and, mopping his face, looked at me with pride. Then he looked above me. His eyes dilated in sheer horror. He gasped, reeled back, and shot out of the room. The door slammed. The sword hanging over the doorframe came unhooked, plunged down, and stabbed the floor. A ripple ran along the blade. For a moment, I watched the sword wobble to and fro, then turned to look behind me. Grandfather stared at me from his portrait. I stared back at him.

If he had made my aunt as sorry a woman as Woldemar suggested, why did she admire him so? He must have taught her something useful too. Was it all those rules about the servants she wanted me to keep in mind? I doubted that all of Grandfather's rules were fair. But if he had told her that the servants were superstitious fools to be afraid of a mere picture, he was proved true just now.

With that in mind, I lifted the bedsheet off the floor, climbed up a chair, and once again covered the portrait.

Дедушкинъ портретъ

CHAPTER TWENTY-SEVEN

In which Prince Lev decides to destroy his unfinished drawing

I stared at the tray they'd brought me, wishing I could share with my mother all these tasty treats. Mother liked her sweets. She had often said her sweet tooth would be her undoing. I wondered which tooth—I would have liked to ask her now. Then again, it would be fun to share the sweets with Vanyousha; a sweet face like his bespoke a sweet tooth, too. But Mother wasn't here yet, and how to find Vanyousha in this enormous house I didn't know, so I had no choice but to eat the sweets myself.

The cream puffs, still warm from the oven, were deli-cious. I polished off three—they melted in my mouth so quickly—and was reaching for the fourth when I spotted a corner of a sheet of paper peeking from beneath the tray. I licked my fingers, wiped them across my jacket front, and pulled the paper out.

It was the sketch of the chamber I had started last night but hadn't had a chance to finish. The fireplace had gone out and then the candles, Vanyousha showed up and then Shysh, and by the time I began my drawings for Mother, I must have mislaid the unfinished sketch some-how. At first, I was disappointed that I had forgotten to complete the drawing. It would've been good for Mother to see where I had been made to spend the night. But after considering the sketch for a moment, I was relieved that Olga Lvovna would not be sending it to Mother.

In the daylight, the drawing seemed eerie. The per-spective was confused, the contours were uncertain, and the shapes at once resembled and disagreed with what was in the room. The panic that I'd felt last night when my

hand did not obey me suddenly returned. How could my hand have gone on drawing without me willing it to draw? That was impossible. Once, I overheard Mother say to someone that on occasion I saw and heard things that simply were not there. I had not believed her then, but I was beginning to believe her now. Last night, scared out of my wits by the sudden darkness, I had imagined that my own hand defied my will.

Better to destroy this wretched drawing, rip it into pieces, and then burn the pieces in the fire. I snatched the sketch and rose quickly. Too quickly. The chamber swirled before my eyes. I felt lightheaded, dropped the sketch, and sunk back into my seat.

Struck by sudden weariness, I laid my cheek against the sketch, inhaling ink and the dusty air of Grandfather's desk. When had I last slept? Was it on the train? Yes, on the train, a long, long time ago.

I closed my lids, and once again I heard the train puffing its way across fields shrouded in snow. Snowdrifts flickered along the tracks, but far away walls of firs stood in the mist like mourners at a funeral. The snow was dotted with crooked crosses and wreaths of rusted tin. In the silence, snowflakes were falling thickly against a marble tombstone. Before the tombstone gaped an open grave, and, next to it, two spades impaled a snowdrift.

CHAPTER TWENTY-EIGHT

*In which Prince Lev challenges
Vanyousha to a duel*

I woke from an explosion of hammers pounding nails into a coffin's lid. I bolted up in panic. The pounding went on, not the hammers but my heart throbbing, bursting out of my chest from the horrific dream. A gray, bleary mist swam before my eyes. I was crying.

"Why did you stop? Keep drawing."

I quickly wiped the tears with my sleeve and looked in the direction of the voice. There was a shape of a darker gray against the grayness of the wall from which a pair of large gray eyes peered at me intently.

"Oh, Vanyousha?" I said. "Is that you?"

He moved away from the wall. "Why did you stop, Your Honor? Keep drawing."

"What do you mean, Vanyousha? I wasn't drawing," I said, and instinctively glanced at the desk before me.

The tray with pies and pancakes and the samovar stood there as before, and as before, the unfinished sketch of Grandfather's chamber lay under the pastry's crumbs. But something wasn't right; the sketch was different. While I was sleeping, someone had advanced the drawing. Grandfather's chair made of antlers had been added, some other objects on the walls, and—my heart jumped when I saw it—a shadow of a human figure slanted hideously across the whole composition.

I looked up at Vanyousha, but he was no longer where I had just seen him. I opened my mouth to call his name when, unexpectedly, he leaned over my shoulder.

"God forgive you!" he cried, snatching the drawing off the desk. "That's not at all what I wanted you to draw!"

"But I didn't draw it, Vanyousha," I said, and at that very instant I saw the blackened pen clasped in my ink-stained fingers.

"Aaah!"

I tossed the pen aside and leaped out of the chair. How awful! Last night my hand had gone on drawing against my will; today it drew while I was sleeping!

"Don't tell a soul," I whispered. "I forbid you."

Vanyousha grinned and tossed the wretched drawing to the floor. "Why would I do that? It's our secret."

"What secret?"

"That you are drawing for me, Your Honor."

"But I only said that I *might* try to draw for you. I didn't yet."

"Yes, you did."

"No, I didn't!"

"Yes, you did."

"Are you calling me a liar?"

He thought about it, glancing at me from time to time and biting at his nails. "Yes," he said at last.

Surely my aunt had a rule regarding such disrespect for my noble position. She would have been very angry with him, but somehow I wasn't. Besides, to be fair, it did seem that I had managed to draw in my sleep. How it happened I simply had no desire to know. Maybe if I tried not to think about my hand having a mind of its own, the horrible thing it was doing might just go away by itself.

"If you're calling me a liar," I announced, "I am challenging you to a duel!"

"To a what?" he said in alarm.

"To a duel. You insulted me, Vanyousha, so I get to choose the weapons."

His face turned paler than it already was. "What weapons?"

"Rapiers!" I sprung up. "Positively rapiers!"

The sword I had played with last night was below the chair. "This one is mine!" I cried, fetching it, and then yanked the sword still stuck in the floor at the threshold. "And this one is yours!" Twirling both blades in the air, I knocked down one candlestick by accident and another one on purpose. "See how it's done?" I cried, laughing, and wheeled round to hand him his sword.

Vanyousha was gone.

"Oh, no!" I cried in frustration. "Not again! Vanyousha? Where are you?"

Silence.

"Vanyousha?"

"Why are you so angry, Your Honor?" His small voice came from someplace in the room.

Thank God he was still here; I was on the verge of tears. A fine new master of Falcon House that would've made me! Bawling my eyes out just because I never had anyone to play with.

"I am not angry, Vanyousha. It's just a game. Come out."

The window drape moved. "What kind of a game?"

"The Three Musketeers, don't you know? One for all and all for one. Please take your sword, Vanyousha. I'll show you how to hold it."

He kept hidden behind the drape but, after a pause, reluctantly held out his hand for the rapier.

CHAPTER TWENTY-NINE

In which Prince Lev and
Vanyousha play musketeers

It took much sweet talk to draw Vanyousha from behind the drape and more sweet talk to convince him to cross swords with me. At every touch of our blades, he scrunched his face, blinked, and skipped back quickly. When I pretended that he pierced my arm, Vanyousha became frightened and hid behind the cabinet.

"You're a fine blade, monsieur!" I cried, changing my sword hand. "But I will slay you still!"

I chased him out of his hiding place and, fighting with

my left, advanced, advanced, advanced. At last I drove him into the corner and, with one terrific blow, kicked the sword out of his grip. He winced and braced himself against the wall. I placed my sword point against his chest.

"Beg for mercy!"

Vanyousha gazed at me. His already huge eyes now seemed twice the size.

"Beg for mercy or I will slay you!"

His lower lip quivered, and his enormous eyes welled up with tears.

"Vanyousha?" I said, lowering my sword. "What's wrong?"

"I don't like this game, Your Honor."

CHAPTER THIRTY

In which Vanyousha reveals a terrible secret

I couldn't tell if Vanyousha was distressed because of losing the fencing bout or because something else was troubling him, but for a long time he sat on the floor with his back to me, pouting. I brought a plate of cream puffs for him, but he refused to try one so I had to eat them all myself. Finally, after much sniffling and sighing and shaking his head in a sorrowful manner, he glanced at me sideways and said, "When you draw for me, Your Honor, draw nice pictures, not like that one." He screwed his eyes toward the unfinished chamber drawing on the floor. "Gentlefolk like to be pleased by pictures. They like to see my mother at a samovar drinking tea, or my uncle making music with wooden spoons, or else a tiny babe playing with a kitty. Sweet things like that. Couldn't you draw those, Your Honor?"

I felt a little sorry for scaring him with my superior fencing, but his request of me was clearly ill fitted. "I only said that I might try to help you, but don't you understand, Vanyousha, it isn't suitable for me to draw such silly things."

"Why not?"

"I have my duties to attend to." And before I could stop myself, I said, "I will be joining the army soon, Vanyousha. They're giving me the rank of general. It's already decided. I'll be a general and a hero like my ancestors, and if you don't know, Vanyousha, heroes do not draw such silly things as someone's mother drinking tea or wooden spoons or kitties. I'm sorry, but I cannot help you. And besides, if you think about it, Vanyousha, helping someone is the same as serving someone."

"So what?"

"So what? Good thing my aunt can't hear you. You're a servant, Vanyousha, and I am a nobleman. I can't be serving servants. You are supposed to serve me instead."

"How can I serve you, Your Honor?" he said eagerly.

"Well, let me think." I rolled my eyes up to the ceiling, and while I pretended to ponder his question, he watched me intently. "What . . . eh . . . what games do you like to play, Vanyousha? If you are scared to play musketeers, we could play pirates instead, or medieval knights, or African explorers."

"Do they have swords too?" he said in his small voice.

What a weakling he really was. I should never have even bothered with someone like him, but if I wanted Vanyousha to play with me, I needed simpler games.

"We could play hide-and-seek, Vanyousha. Or would you rather play tag? This house is great for running. It's so big, and there are so many safe places to hide in."

"Not so safe, Your Honor."

"Why not?"

"Some rooms are haunted."

I laughed. "Last night you took me for a spirit."

"How could I not? This house is full of spooks."

"Have you seen them?"

"Saw them with my own eyes. Heard them too."

"What do they say?"

"They say things." He glanced round fearfully and moved in closer. " 'Are you there, little boy?' " he groaned in a ghostly voice. " 'Speak to us, speak to us.' "

A strange glare appeared in his eyes that made me feel uneasy, and I too glanced round fearfully. "They say that?"

"They do. But that's not the worst of it."

"What's the worst of it?"

"It's a terrible, terrible secret, Your Honor. God will strike you dead if you tell."

"I won't tell, I swear."

He moved in closer still. "Say it—'Let God strike me dead if I tell.' "

"Let God strike me dead if I tell," I whispered.

"Listen, then," he said, and moved even closer. "They have a room in this house as small as a box to bury the dead in."

"A coffin?"

"Yes." He nodded. "A coffin."

Our faces were so close now that both of Vanyousha's huge eyes merged into one gigantic gray eye with a restlessly quivering glare.

"Such noises come from that room, your blood curdles. But there's more. That room won't stay in place. I've seen folks go in and lock the door, and the room snatches them away. When the room goes up, folk go to heaven, but when the room goes down, it takes them to hell. God is my witness!"

I laughed so hard that I stumbled, fell against the wall, and slid to the floor.

"What so funny?"

"It's an elevator, Vanyousha! Don't you know what an elevator is?"

"A what?"

"It's a machine made to take people up and down between the floors, so they don't have to walk the stairs."

Vanyousha regarded me with a mocking grin.

"What?" I said, ceasing laughing at once. "You don't believe me?"

"It's whatever you say, Your Honor. You're to be a general soon. You must know."

"Yes, I do," I said, trying to conceal my frustration with the ignorant boy. "We shall play tag now, Vanyousha. Come, let's begin."

CHAPTER THIRTY-ONE

In which Prince Lev fails to tag Vanyousha

Vanyousha was incredibly fast. He ducked into side doors, sped through long passages, disappeared behind furnishings, and reappeared in the most unexpected places. I was out of breath from trying to tag him.

Once, chasing him across a vast and murky room with creaky parquet floors and blurry mirrors—probably a ballroom—I came right behind Vanyousha and reached with my hand to tag him. Vanyousha ducked under my hand and wheeled round, and when I looked behind me, he was gone. Along the walls stood rows of chairs draped under gray, dusty covers. I studied them for any movement. Nothing stirred. All was still save for the muted clinking of the chandeliers inside their canvas wrappings. When I glimpsed their reflection in the mirrored walls, I felt uneasy. In the clouded glass, the covered chandeliers suspended from the ceiling looked like men with bags over their heads hanged by their necks.

"Your Honor?" Vanyousha appeared suddenly, as if out of nowhere. "Why did you stop playing? Come and get me!"

The reflection of his white shirt streaked across the mirrors as he darted out of the ballroom. I chased him through the double doors into the next salon, but I halted there once again, not at all amused. I could have sworn Vanyousha wasn't anywhere in the room, and yet I felt distinctly that someone's eyes were watching me. Cautiously, I peered about.

On the somber walls, the death masks of my forefathers hung in eerie silence. Gray with dust, their lids were tightly drawn over their sunken eyes, and still I felt their chilly gaze upon me.

"I'm here!" Vanyousha's voice sprung from behind my back.

Startled, I spun round. "I don't like this game, Vanyousha."

"You don't?" he said, surprised. "I know a better one. Do you like sledding down icy hills?"

"What?"

He skipped a little in delight. "Follow me, Your Honor."

I must have blinked, because I missed Vanyousha darting toward the door. He was already there. "Follow, Your Honor!" he called, running out.

The air of the room quivered with the echo of his voice. The sound was so near and so distinct, it seemed that it wasn't Vanyousha but rather my forefathers calling to me from the walls.

CHAPTER THIRTY-TWO

In which Prince Lev rides down the banister

I chased after Vanyousha through a long succession of rooms. Their opened doorways, perfectly lined up and reduced by perspective, seemed to continue forever. Ahead of me, Vanyousha ran through doorway after doorway, now appearing close, now far away, as if to tease me. No matter how fast I ran I could not catch up with him. The farthest room opened onto a staircase landing, and there Vanyousha halted and suddenly rose slightly in midair. I burst onto the landing and saw him perched atop the wrought-iron banister. Vanyousha smiled, waved for me to follow, and plunged down the polished handrail's curve.

I leaped upon the banister and nearly tumbled head over heels, but I caught the handrail and saved my balance. Without hesitation, I leaned my shoulders forward, let go of the handrail, and, like a shot out of a pistol, flew after Vanyousha into a bottomless abyss.

My heart stopped beating. Maybe to Vanyousha this was like sliding down icy hills, but to me it felt like a ride to death. The banister wove left and right, chilled air lashed my face, wind howled in my ears, and floor after floor merged into one flying streak. At every turn I was terrified that I'd be hurled off the banister, but somehow the handrail held me. Held me! What fun! I spiraled down, wishing that Falcon House had twenty, fifty, a hundred floors more to slide past. But then, Vanyousha's tiny figure appeared far below. He waved his arms as if to greet me or to warn me. His body swiftly grew, and in a moment I was about to smash into him. He darted out of the way. The handrail curved away from under me. Launched into the air, I flew across the landing. A marble wall lunged at me. I smacked against it, but it didn't hurt at all. Laughing, I spun round to Vanyousha, but he was gone. Instead it was Olga Lvovna peering at me in astonishment.

CHAPTER THIRTY-THREE

*In which Prince Lev learns
about the Corps des Pages*

"If I may be so bold, Prince," said Olga Lvovna after a moment of painful silence, "may I inquire what you are doing?"

I stood up, rubbing my bruised elbow. "Nothing."

"Nothing?" she echoed, startled, and turned her lorgnette on Woldemar, who had wheeled her onto the landing at the very moment I smashed into the wall. "Did he say *nothing*, Woldemar?"

"Yes, madam," Woldemar confirmed. "Nothing."

Княжна Ольга Львовна

By the manner in which Woldemar was biting his lips and refusing to look in my direction, I could tell he was struggling to suppress a laugh.

"It is my duty to inform you, Prince," said Olga Lvovna, "that what I just had the misfortune to witness was hardly nothing."

I hung my head low to show her how ashamed I was, but in truth, I too was afraid to catch Woldemar's eye and burst out laughing.

"Your grandfather, whom you chose as your role model," continued Olga Lvovna with a dignified air, "imposed on me certain obligations, the most important of which is to uphold the honor of our family. I have dedicated my entire life to fulfilling his wishes, and I will not allow anyone—including you, Prince—to taint the spotless reputation of Falcon House."

There was a silly giggle from Woldemar. Olga Lvovna spun round, whipping the lorgnette to her eyes, but by the time she glared at him, Woldemar was standing at attention with the most serious expression on his face. While she eyed him with suspicion, I couldn't stop myself and giggled too. The lorgnette swooshed in my direction.

"What's so funny, Prince?"

"Nothing."

"Nothing again!" Exasperated, she thwacked the handle of her lorgnette against the armrest of the wheelchair. "I'm shocked that a boy of your birth and breeding should find it necessary to engage in such unseemly behavior. Return to your grandfather's study at once."

"No," I said.

She glared at me in utter shock. "What do you mean, no?"

"I don't want to go back to my room, Aunt," I said, amazed at my own audacity. "It's boring. And it's dusty."

"Dusty?"

"Yes, it's dusty, and it's too quiet. Why do you want me always to be in that room?"

"There are reasons," she blurted out.

"What reasons?"

She opened her mouth to reply but did not speak and slowly closed her lips, which formed a thin, unpleasant line again. Then came a lengthy silence.

I listened to her fingernails drumming the armrest of her chair and thought how lucky Vanyousha was to be a fast runner. What awful trouble he'd be in if she had run into him instead of me.

"I have it!" exclaimed Olga Lvovna triumphantly. "What you're supposed to do in your grandfather's study, my dear Prince, is to prepare for your examinations."

"What examinations?"

"To the Corps des Pages,[9] Prince, what else?"

"The boarding school?"

"Russia's best! How else will you become . . . how did you put it? A hero and a general?"

"I have to go to a boarding school for that?"

"Do you plan to become the master of this house, my dear, by sliding down banisters?" she said ironically. "Please pay attention. You will be tested on the following:

Divine Law, Arithmetic, French, and Russian. I remember clearly, my poor brother failed all four. Admittance was refused to him, and look what happened."

"What happened?"

"He amounted to nothing. But Daddy! Oh, Daddy passed his exams with flying colors. Flying colors, Prince! And that is why he went on to have a brilliant career and was well received at the court of our late emperor. Isn't that what you desire?"

I thought about it. "Yes," I said.

"A wise decision, Prince," she said, clearly relieved, and looked me up and down through her lorgnette. "Woldemar?"

"Yes, madam?"

"Isn't this the same gloomy suit that Prince wore upon his arrival?"

He peered at my suit for a moment. "Yes, madam."

"Don't you have any other clothes, Prince?" she said.

"I don't know," I replied. "Mother might have packed some."

The instant the words were out of my mouth, I regretted having shown such dependence on my mother. Olga Lvovna must have noticed it, for she glanced at me with sympathy.

"Do not be concerned, Prince. I will arrange for appropriate attire for you to wear. I do have a costume in mind. But for now, return to your chamber. You must study. I will have the required books delivered at once."

CHAPTER THIRTY-FOUR

In which Vanyousha interrupts
Prince Lev's studies

If I had known that I had to go to a boarding school to learn how to rule Falcon House, I might not have left my mother's side. The truth is, I had never attended school before, since Mother herself had taught me at home. At the boarding school they would have much harsher teachers than Mother, and besides, I would have to sleep in a dorm. It would not be any worse, of course, than sleeping in my grandfather's chamber. At least there would be other boys around—noblemen like me, not just silly servants like Vanyousha. But what if I got sick? Petersburg was so cold, I could easily catch an infection. They would probably let Mother know, but would they let her take care of me in the dorm?

My father hadn't gone to the boarding school, and he had amounted to nothing. He was too soft, said Olga Lvovna. I wondered what she meant by that. Regardless, I had little choice in the matter if I wanted to follow in the steps of my role model. Grandfather had passed his tests with flying colors, gone on to have a brilliant career, and been well received at court. Wouldn't that be marvelous, to be well received at court? To see our emperor the Tsar in real life, instead of in the picture I copied into my drawing album? Vanyousha said that he had seen the Tsar. Vanyousha was a liar. But what is shameful in a servant is more shameful in a master. Was I not a liar, too, by telling him that I'd be joining the army soon in the rank of a general? Why did I say that? Why was I even wasting my time with Vanyousha? My aunt is right. I won't become the master of this house by sliding down banisters!

A stack of old, dusty books was waiting outside my chamber's door. I brought them in and spread the books upon the desk: French and Russian, Arithmetic and Divine Law, all the subjects Olga Lvovna said I would be tested on.

I hesitated, deciding which book to open first. Not that it mattered; it shouldn't be too hard for me to pass what was required. French I didn't need to study; I already knew it. Of course, *En garde! Prêts? Allez!* were the only words I knew, but they were the most important words in French—you couldn't start fencing without saying them. I didn't have to bother with the Russian grammar, either. Russian is my mother tongue, and besides, I write in cursive neatly. Well, almost neatly. As for Arithmetic . . . true, numbers had always troubled me a little. But I could draw them well—zeroes in particular. Divine Law was the thickest book of all and likely the most boring. I didn't even want to open it. But as I sat, gazing at the cover of the book—a golden cross stamped into black leather—I came to understand that Divine Law was the book I needed most. That book was full of miracles, and short of a

miracle, I would not pass my exams with flying colors like my grandfather had. In truth, I was unlikely to pass them at all.

With a groan, I opened the book and dust erupted from the pages in a thick gray cloud. I sneezed.

"God bless, Your Honor."

I looked up quickly. Vanyousha was standing beside the desk.

"Ah, it's you!" I said, displeased, and began reading.

"You couldn't tag me."

I ignored his comment.

"Your Honor? I was faster."

I kept on reading, determined to take no notice of him.

"Your Honor?"

"What?" I nearly shouted. "Can't you see I am busy? Please go away."

He looked at me in alarm but didn't move. I shook my head to make it clear how annoying his presence was and went back to reading.

"The flying coffin is still there, Your Honor."

I didn't answer, and he fell silent. After I waited long enough, I stole a glance at him. With his flaxen head cocked to one side, Vanyousha, looking past me, was listening to something. "It's on its way to heaven now," he said at last.

I listened. Not a sound.

"And now it's dropping down to hell."

"Don't you have any duties to attend to?" I said.

He glanced at me uneasily.

"Be so kind as to remove yourself from my study," I ordered, "and go do something useful instead of standing around listening to the elevator going up and down."

"It's a coffin."

"It's an elevator!"

"A coffin."

"Argh!" I cried angrily, and slammed the book shut. A cloud of dust rose again. I sneezed.

"God bless, Your Honor."

"Please go away, Vanyousha," I pleaded. "It is not a coffin. It is an elevator. E-le-va-tor, don't you understand? One day I'll show you."

"Now, Your Honor?"

"No, Vanyousha, not now! Can't you see I have important things to do?"

I opened the book and tried to study, but it was hopeless to ponder the divine laws under Vanyousha's pleading gaze. Besides, those laws had been printed so closely together, the tiny letters merged, forming wavy lines. The lines swam fast before my eyes, blurring into one madly flying streak. At once, I was reminded of what fun it had been to slide down the handrail with Vanyousha.

"Are you scared of the flying coffin?" he said right near me.

I looked up quickly. Vanyousha was not where he had stood before but right beside my chair.

"Scared?" I said, pretending that his sudden shifts in space did not alarm me. "Of the elevator? Why should I be scared?" I tossed the book aside. "I've been riding them for years."

CHAPTER THIRTY-FIVE

In which Prince Lev and Vanyousha ride down to hell

It took a long time for Vanyousha to gather courage to enter the elevator cage, but I tried hard to refrain from mocking him and waited patiently. When finally he entered, I stepped in after him, shut the door, and in response, the floor swayed under our feet. Vanyousha gasped and braced himself against the latticed wall.

"How brave you are, Vanyousha!" I couldn't stop myself from saying, but glancing at his frightened face,

I regretted my sarcastic remark. Embarrassed, I quickly turned away from him to busy myself with three cast-iron levers protruding from the wall. Woldemar had used these levers to set the cage in motion. Along the grooves in which the levers moved ran rows of numbers. I did not know what those numbers stood for or which lever made the cage go up and which one down.[10]

"Where are we heading, Your Honor?" Vanyousha whispered. "Down to hell or up to heaven?"

"Be patient. You'll know in a minute."

With a confident air, I shifted the first lever down a few notches, but nothing happened. I glanced at Vanyousha, who, pressing his back against the wall, was gazing at me, wide-eyed. I shifted the second lever. The bell rang out and the cage began to rattle. Vanyousha's eyes got bigger. I shifted the third lever. With a jolt and a screech, the cage began inching down.

"To hell," Vanyousha said in a desperate voice.

"This is the first lifting machine in Saint Petersburg,

Vanyousha. My grandfather built it at great expense to impress the emperor."

"Our Lord Jesus Christ, Holy Mother of God," Vanyousha began in a whisper, rapidly crossing himself.

"I wonder if the emperor was impressed, though. It's a little slow, don't you think?"

"Father, Son, and Holy Ghost, Our Lord—"

"Don't be silly, Vanyousha, we are perfectly safe."

Vanyousha uttered a moan and, clasping his hands together, fell to his knees. "Don't take me to hell, Your Honor, I beg of you!"

"I must say, Vanyousha, this is a little annoying. I was very busy studying for my examinations, but you insisted on riding the elevator. So here we are, riding it."

"Please, please, Your Honor! I can't die without seeing my mama first."

"Stop talking about your mother all the time!"

"Mama!" Vanyousha cried suddenly. "Maaaaa- maaaaaaa!"

I wheeled round to slap my hand over his screaming

mouth, but just then, the floor of the cage whacked against something hard. I clutched the latticework to keep my balance. We'd come to a stop. My back was to the door, and when I heard it open, I spun—but Vanyousha had already vanished from the cage.

CHAPTER THIRTY-SIX

In which hell smells like mothballs

Above, a distant light washed over the dilapidated walls, fading by the time it reached the bottom. I groped my way out of the cage and entered a sealed granite vault, dark and chilly, with moisture glistening upon its stonework.

"Vanyousha? Where are you?"

The echo of my whisper quivered between the somber walls as something scurried at my feet. I leaped aside.

A sliver of yellowish light glowed through a chink in

the uneven floor. As I approached, I saw a trapdoor. Bands of rusted metal, crude iron clamps, and heavy nails held the worm-eaten hatch with no ring to lift it open. I looked around. Besides the trapdoor, the vault had no other exits. Where did Vanyousha go?

I squeezed my fingers between the hatch and the stone floor, grasped the rotting planks from below, and lifted the hatch. The rusted hinges groaned. While the hatch stood angled over the hole in the floor, it resembled the yawning jaws of some monstrous beast. What a stench rose from there! I reeled back in disgust. The hatch arced away from me and with a loud bang crashed against the stone floor. The putrid odor that had seeped into every room of Falcon House swelled up from that very hole. Perhaps Vanyousha was not mistaken—only hell could stink this much.

Pinching my nose so as not to smell the horrid stench, I leaned into the trapdoor. Below me, a stone staircase spiraled down in ever-narrowing circles, farther and farther, until it disappeared in the dark. Had Vanyousha run down those steps? But why then was the hatch closed? I hesitated, knowing that the proper thing to do was to ride the elevator back up to my floor and return to my studies. But how could I abandon Vanyousha in such a wretched place? He was so easily scared.

I lowered myself through the trapdoor until my feet reached the slippery staircase and stepped cautiously down. The lower I descended, the more intolerable the stench became. Soon I felt so dizzy, I had to stop. Panting, I leaned my forehead against a clammy wall and, in that instant, recognized the smell.

At home, Mother had kept my father's garments in a trunk. In secret, I often took them out and tried them on before a mirror. His clothes smelled of mothballs, just as the air about me now smelled, but here the smell of mothballs merged with something else, some decaying matter. Was this the place that Woldemar had called *the mothballs?* He had said to keep away from this place. If Olga Lvovna found out that I—

Летучие Мыши

With a piercing shriek, something burst up from the steps below. I ducked a slashing wing. All at once, shrieks and a beating of wings reverberated through the passage. I swatted at the mob of bats and bolted down the stairs.

CHAPTER THIRTY-SEVEN

In which the old valet is about to be thrown out

The spiral staircase dropped me into a stone cellar. Below an oppressively low ceiling, a tightly packed mass of blackened rags hung from the crossbars. As I descended to the floor and took a close look at those rags, I saw that they were not rags at all but army uniforms of the highest ranks. The tunics, capes, and greatcoats dating back to the times of the great Tsar Peter[11] had once been cut from the finest cloth trimmed in gold, but now they were fouled by mold. The stench of mothballs and decaying matter that spread through the entire house oozed off these garments.

No sign yet of Vanyousha in the cellar, but farther up a light flickered, a shadow moved across the ceiling, and someone squeaked, "Feel the wool here, brother. Look at this stitching. It's a sin to ruin it."

I moved toward the voice through a narrow aisle, cringing every time damp, rotting cloth flapped against my face.

"Cut it up, she says, so it fits him like a glove," the squeaky voice went on. "I ought to measure the boy, but does she let me? No, she says, it's a surprise. What surprise? That I'm tearing up his grandfather's best parade dress?"

At last, I made my way toward the back wall of the cellar. There, lit by a single candle, a small man in wire-rimmed glasses hovered over a crimson-and-gold tunic laid out on the workbench before him. Unmistakably, the man was an experienced tailor: he cut the tunic with scissors, marked it with chalk, and stuck it with pins with such speed, his hands seemed to blur in the flickering light of the candle. Across from the tailor sat the old valet Shysh. With his toothless mouth open and his chin tucked into the dirty shirtfront, Shysh was asleep.

As I moved aside a hanging overcoat, the decayed garment disintegrated at my touch and shreds of it fell to the floor. The tailor gave a start, and the pins he clenched between his teeth dropped out of his mouth.

"Hey, brother," he squeaked, squinting in my direction. "There's someone there!"

Shysh stirred, shivered, and slowly turned round. He looked much worse since the time I saw him in Grandfather's chamber. His shriveled, yellowish skin looked transparent and, as he peered into the dark, his left eye quivered with nervous twitches.

I was about to reveal myself so as not to alarm them when heavy stomping shook the floor behind me. Someone was coming up the aisle. I darted out of the way. A large figure lumbered past.

Лукинъ

Портной

Шишка

There was a sound of a scuffle, a chair fell, and someone growled, "Got him!" I peeked out from behind the mildewed cloak. The doorman, Lukich, stood by the workbench, holding Shysh suspended in the air by the collar of his tailcoat. The old man's feet dangled helplessly above the floor and he was choking.

"Collect your things," Lukich growled. "Your time with us is over."

"Leave him be, brother," squeaked the tailor. "What's the harm in him?"

Keeping Shysh hanging with one hand, Lukich stuck his enormous fist under the tailor's nose. "And what's the harm in this . . . brother?"

I felt terribly ashamed. The voice within me commanded me to rush at Lukich and, if required, fight him. After all, I had caused this trouble for Shysh. I was to blame. Besides, my duty as a nobleman was to protect my servants. I must prevent that nasty brute from tossing the old man out to certain death.

And yet I hesitated. The brute Lukich looked terrifying.

Just then, someone dashed out in front of me. Vanyousha's eyes glittered in the dark.

"Watch this, Your Honor."

CHAPTER THIRTY-EIGHT

In which Vanyousha disguises himself

What happened next was as extraordinary as it was comical. Vanyousha stepped into the light, disguised beneath some of the foul garments kept in the cellar. An ancient tunic with one missing epaulet and no buttons concealed his whole figure, a dented hussar's helmet sat cockeyed on his head, and on his feet he wore a pair of broken-down riding boots, split at the seams and many times his size. He stuck his arms out like a scarecrow, clomped up to Lukich, swayed a little, and let out a long and mournful sigh.

Lukich was still holding his fist under the tailor's nose, and Shysh still dangled from his other hand, and in that peculiar statue-like pose, all three men gaped in absolute horror at Vanyousha.

Vanyousha stomped one boot against the floor. Lukich winced. Vanyousha stomped the other boot. The tailor whimpered. Moaning, Vanyousha began twirling in place. Round and round he went, slowly at first, then faster, faster, soon spinning like a top. As he spun, the tunic's sleeves, which were much too long for him, floated up in the air and slapped Lukich in the face. Lukich leaped back in horror, dropping Shysh to the floor like a sack of bones.

I stepped out in the aisle just as Lukich took to his heels. Wailing, he ran straight into me and shoved me aside. I went down, snatching at the hanging cloaks. They splintered and burst off their hangers. One foul garment after another piled onto me. I thrashed violently to free myself, but the more I thrashed, the more entangled I became. Wrapped up like a mummy in noxious strands of cloth, I rolled round the floor. I was losing strength, but I kept on struggling, knowing that I had no right to choke to death right now. If I died, there would be no one left to rule Falcon House.

At that moment, I felt the rags begin to loosen, as if someone were trying to free me of the foul bondage. At last, I managed to sit up, gasping and wheezing and coughing up bile. Laughing, Vanyousha stood over me. When at last I got my breath, I said, "It's not funny," and ordered him to stop.

But he couldn't. Tears came into his eyes, and, shaking from laughter, he collapsed to the floor beside me. I glanced at him with contempt, then with dignity, and finally with pleasure. Previously, in my chamber, I had laughed at him, and now Vanyousha, still in his demented disguise, was having the same laugh at me. Before I knew it, the two of us were howling together like madmen.

CHAPTER THIRTY-NINE

In which Prince Lev and Vanyousha fly up to heaven

The servants must have fled the cellar while I struggled under the rotten coats. Vanyousha and I were alone. After laughing our heads off, we sat side by side on the floor, grinning foolishly. Vanyousha didn't seem to be bothered by the horrid stench, but I was. Besides, all that choking and laughing had given me a bad case of hiccups.

"Do you want to see my mother?" he suddenly asked.

I glared at him and opened my mouth to answer, but a hiccup came out instead. He laughed.

"Take me up to heaven in the coffin, Your Honor, and I'll show you."

Poor boy, he still believed that the elevator was a coffin running up and down between heaven and hell. I shrugged. "If you wish, Vanyousha."

"Bless your heart, Your Honor!"

He leaped to his feet and bounded up the stairs ahead of me.

Strangely, Vanyousha's former fear of the elevator had passed; he rushed right into the cage, looked to see if I was following, and called excitedly, "Come, come, Your Honor!"

I entered after him, and when I turned to shut the door, he cried behind my back, "Let us go fast!"

I spun round just as Vanyousha was about to take hold of one of the levers. "Don't touch the levers!" I shouted.

He leaped back, frightened.

"Never touch these," I said sternly. "You do not know how"—a hiccup interrupted me—"to work them." And to show him how well I knew, in one quick, foolish move I thrust the lever up past all the numbers.

There was a terrific noise. The cage shook, rattled, and all at once shot up with lightning speed. Thrown off my feet, I rolled across the floor and banged into the wall. Vanyousha screamed so piercingly, the lamp exploded into a million glass fragments. Now in the dark, the cage continued to charge up the shaft, lurching from side to side and scraping at the walls. With every grinding noise, fiery sparks burst in through the open latticed walls. Smoke began filling up the cage. The floor throbbed so much, I was forced to crawl to reach the levers. I tried and tried but couldn't draw down the lever I had so recklessly engaged. The wretched thing was stuck.

I hauled myself up to my feet and looked out. The cage was flying past one of the landings where Lukich, surrounded by open-mouthed servants, was spinning in place in a poor imitation of Vanyousha's trick in the cellar. When the cage shrieked by, the servants scrambled away, but Lukich hesitated just long enough to catch my eye.

Я и Ванюша поднимаемся на лифте

One landing after another flickered by. I didn't want Vanyousha to see that I was also frightened, so I began counting the floors. Besides, I had always wanted to find out how tall Falcon House was in order to draw a proper picture of it for my mother.

"Ten ... eleven ... twelve ... thirteen ..."

"What are you doing?" wailed Vanyousha. "Can't you see? We are going to die!"

"Nonsense, Vanyou—"

Just then, the top of the cage rammed into something. The ceiling exploded. Sharp as arrows, wooden splinters shot at us from above. The cage door burst off its hinges and crashed flat out onto the landing. I leaped out of the cage and wheeled round.

"Get out of there!" I shouted, but I couldn't see Vanyousha in the cage through all the smoke.

There was a loud crack at the top of the shaft, and a cast-iron pulley tumbled into the cage. All of the grinding and screeching suddenly ceased, and the cage swayed in silence. I hiccupped. Something snapped in the dark, and with a howling shriek, the cage plummeted down the shaft.

"Vanyoushaaaaaaaa!"

I was on my belly at the edge of the landing when Vanyousha appeared beside me.

"Clever boy," I said, grinning at him. "You made it out!"

Together we leaned over the edge and looked down into the shaft. Frayed steel cables, ripped from holding the cage, flailed about, smacking the walls. The cage was still falling, becoming smaller and smaller until it was swallowed by darkness. There was a terrific crash. The whole house shuddered. In an instant, an earsplitting shriek echoed through the shaft. A boiling black cloud rose from below, screeching, shape-shifting, and cartwheeling right at us.

I sprang away from the opening. Bats poured out of the shaft, swooping across the landing in a thick, black smudge. I shut my eyes, feeling the air vibrate with their frenzied flight. I waited until the shrieks died down before I dared to raise my lids. Vanyousha stood beside me, grinning.

"Come, Your Honor. I'll show you my mother."

CHAPTER FORTY

*In which Prince Lev and Vanyousha
wish upon a star*

I climbed after Vanyousha through an attic window onto a roof that slanted sharply under a coat of glassy ice. It was dark already and bitter cold. Ice crystals shimmered in the frosty air, pricking my face like needles. I took a deep breath and slowly exhaled a cloud of dense steam. I had arrived at Falcon House only the night before, but it seemed I had not breathed fresh air in weeks.

Below us in the waiting stillness gleamed Saint Petersburg. The churches, palaces, and bridges lay buried under the brilliance of snow. The sky shone with stars. Their pale blue flicker reflected from the frozen river that sliced the city into islands like shards of a shattered mirror.[12]

"My village is beyond the river," said Vanyousha. "Can you see it?"

I looked in the direction he was pointing, but past the river was just blackness.

"Mother's hut is behind those birches. See the roof made of straw?"

I glanced at him out of the corner of my eye. "Yes," I lied. "I see it."

"Mother has a lovely hut. It's white as milk inside, the oven's always warm, and it smells good in there—lived in." He started a smile, but instead he frowned. "See my mother in the window? She's crying. Ever since they carried me away from her, Mother has been crying." Vanyousha sniffled and wiped his nose on his shirtsleeve. "I'd rather be dead, Your Honor, than be away from her."

"Stop calling me Your Honor. My name is Lev."

He looked at me but didn't reply. Somewhere down below, a solitary church bell began a mournful toll. We stood without talking and listened to the tolling of the bell and watched the stars. All of the stars were different. Some seemed to be made of gold but some of silver; some were blue but some were purple; some stars were bright but some were faint; some were far away, some close; and some blinked fast, while others only now and then.

"How beautiful," I said. "I wish I knew how to draw these stars."

"Try it," Vanyousha said. "Your picture will come out pretty."

"How do you know?"

"I just know, Levushka," he said with a mischievous smile.

Levushka? That was what Mother always called me. Not Prince or Lev but Levushka, in a kindly way.

"If you wish upon a shooting star," he said, "your wish comes true."

"You believe that?"

"I do, but you have to keep your wish a secret."

He turned away and peered up into the sky. Stars pulsated in the frosty air, as if keeping time with the tolling of the bell. Minutes passed, but not one of the stars fell. Vanyousha sighed and looked away.

"Can you see your mother from here?"

"No, Vanyousha, she's too far away. But I will see her soon."

"Soon?" he echoed, and glanced at me with envy. "When?"

"First I have to become the master of this house like my grandfather was, and then—"

"Look!" he cried, pointing up. "A shooting star!"

A shooting star, such as I had never seen the likes of, stood in the sky, trembling faintly. Instead of moving, its tail arched over the city like a golden bridge. At intervals, the tail swelled to the brightest burn, then waned slowly, as if the star were sighing for some poor soul. At last, the tail began to fade, became translucent, and expired, but its afterglow shimmered in the inky sky.

"I made a wish," Vanyousha said. "I . . ." Eager to continue, he parted his pale lips to speak, but after a glance at me, he halted. Carefully, he closed his lips, but they refused to stay in place and spread into a smile. "Did you make a wish?"

I nodded.

"Good," he said. "Good, Levushka."

"Levushka," I echoed, smiling, and shook my head at him. "So what are we going to tell Olga Lvovna about that elevator, Vanyousha? She'll be awfully angry."

His eyes became alarmed. "Who will be angry?"

"Don't worry," I said. "I'll be the one responsible. Lukich did not see you in the cage. You won't be punished."

"I was punished once," he said, and his face darkened. "Made me so sick, I near died."

"How were you punished?"

"Flogged."

"Flogged? For what?"

"I couldn't draw pictures, remember?" He bit his lip and glanced at me. "Want to see?"

"See what?"

He turned his back to me and rolled his shirt up to his shoulders.

"Good God!" I gasped, horror-struck.

Vanyosha's white, slender back was one horrific wound, densely gouged with deep, intersecting grooves.

"Your Excellency!" someone cried. "Thank heavens! You're alive!"

I turned to the sound of the voice and saw Woldemar climbing out of the attic window. When I looked back, Vanyousha was no longer near me. I spotted him in a deep shadow against the chimney's wall. When our eyes met, he pressed a finger to his lips and smiled.

"Careful, Your Excellency, it is unsafe up here!" cried Woldemar, cautiously moving over the icy roof and holding his hand out to me. "We feared that you had fallen in with the elevator. Madam is beside herself."

CHAPTER FORTY-ONE

*In which Prince Lev questions his aunt
and receives an unexpected answer*

The moment Woldemar ushered me into Olga Lvovna's chamber, she burst into a flood of tears. "You may feel pleased at your work, Prince Lev," she groaned from behind her tear-soaked handkerchief. "Instead of preparing for your examinations, you torment me by putting your life in danger—climbing roofs, sliding down banisters, and riding runaway elevators. After all that I have done for you, Prince, why do you punish me?"

I could feel color rising to my cheeks and my fists

clenching, but I would not reveal how furious I was at her.

"It is not I but you, Aunt, who punishes people," I said as coolly as I could manage. "I was not aware that flogging is still allowed."

She started and lowered her handkerchief. "What?"

"Flogging, Aunt," I repeated. "Flogging servants has not been allowed since our Tsar gave them freedom."

She paused, gazing at me with a surprised lift of her eyebrow. "Giving them freedom hardly came to any good," said she at last. "The servants have no use for it. But kindly tell me, Prince, whom did I supposedly flog?"

"Please, stop pretending, Aunt. You know perfectly well that you ordered Vanyousha flogged."

"Who's Vanyousha?"

"Aunt! Vanyousha is a boy in your service."

"Wait a minute, Prince—"

"No! I will not wait!" I cried, stomping my foot. "How could you do such a horrible thing to a little boy?"

She smiled, as if she actually enjoyed seeing me angry.

"But I do not have boys in my service, my dear. Neither do I have girls. I forbid my servants to marry, hence no children."

"Do you expect me to believe this? Why would anyone forbid people to marry?"

"Your grandfather did not allow his servants to marry, and neither do I," she said, shrugging her shoulders. "I do not question the rules I inherited from Daddy but endeavor to faithfully follow them. I was hoping you would do the same, Prince."

"But . . . but what about Vanyousha? I don't understand."

"Neither do I, Prince. Do you, Woldemar?"

Woldemar crimsoned and didn't reply.

"Answer me, villain!"

"No, madam."

"No, what?"

"I don't understand, madam."

"See, Prince? No one understands," Olga Lvovna concluded with satisfaction. "If I recall correctly, you claimed to have seen a boy upon your arrival here. Am I to assume that it's the same boy? You have spoken with him and he has told you that he was flogged?" Her black eyes, fixed steadily upon my face, shone with excitement. "How frequently does this happen to you, Prince? Do you often see boys who are not there?"

I gazed at her in utter confusion. In spite of my accusations, she seemed to understand how I felt and spoke to me kindly. "Do not be alarmed, dear boy. I promise that I will keep this a secret. No one will know." She glared at Woldemar. "Did you hear, villain? Don't breathe a word to anyone."

"Yes, madam."

She peered back at me. "Trust me, Prince, you will be rewarded for the misfortunes that befell you. I will make sure of that. Do you still desire to follow in your grandfather's footsteps? Still want to be the master of this house?"

I was so confused about Vanyousha that I could hardly follow her questions, but she pressed on. "Did you begin studying for your entry exams to the Corps des Pages?"

I peered at her, unable to utter a sound.

She gave a little nod. "I understand completely. I saw your poor father struggling with all those superfluous subjects. But do not worry, my dear, your aunt has thought of everything."

She beckoned me with her finger, and when, after some hesitation, I stepped closer, she whispered, "Listen carefully, Prince. Tonight you will meet someone in whose hands lies your future. He and I were very close in our youth, closer than I care to admit." She batted her eyelashes like a little girl but instantly checked herself. "But that is beside the point. This virtuous and profound man has always been a benefactor to our family. One word from him, and your exams for the Corps des Pages will be a mere formality." Her face lit up with a bright smile unusual for her. "You won't even have to study. Aren't you pleased?"

I didn't know if I was pleased or not. All I could think about was Vanyousha, but she was being so nice to me that I felt I had to say something. "Sorry about your elevator, Aunt," I said. "It was an accident."

"Do not blame yourself, my dear. It is entirely my fault. I should never have allowed you to wander the house on your own. Too much freedom is not good for anyone." She turned to Woldemar. "Listen to me, villain. Find a reliable man to serve Prince Lev as his valet, someone quick-witted and vigilant to keep him from harm. Do we have such a man?"

"Shysh is good," I put in quickly. "I want Shysh."

Olga Lvovna frowned and glanced at Woldemar with suspicion. "I will consider your request, Prince, but I make no promises. For now, Woldemar will escort you to your room." She scrutinized me through her lorgnette for a moment. "As I mentioned, that gloomy suit of yours must go. I have ordered you a garment befitting the occasion. Prepare yourself to be at your best, my dear. Your future will be decided tonight."

CHAPTER FORTY-TWO

In which Prince Lev cracks the whip

The explanation that I received from Olga Lvovna had left me so utterly lost, bewildered, and alone that I missed my mother more than ever. I longed to have Mother by my side, to have her look into my eyes and hold my hand as she had always done when consoling me about some trifle. But this was no trifle! Who Vanyousha was, where he had come from, and who had dared such violence against him was a mystery. Only Mother could have helped me solve it.

And so as before, I sat behind my grandfather's dusty desk, and as before, instead of writing words I was drawing pictures. It was the only way I knew how to speak to Mother now.

Why did she tell me not to follow the rules? I failed to follow Olga Lvovna's rules and succeeded only in causing a lot of trouble. And what was it about drawing from my heart? Oh, what did it matter? My sketches now came with no effort, as if my hand knew what and how to draw without me even trying. The picture of the stars above the city that I never thought I could draw had turned out pretty, just as Vanyousha had promised. I must ask Olga Lvovna to send this picture to Mother at once; how amazed Mother will be at my newfound skill.

While I was sketching, the recollections of my conversation with Olga Lvovna turned in my mind. She said that Vanyousha wasn't in her service, but truth be told, he'd never said he was. What was he doing in her house then, and how was he getting in? Not through the front door. That brute Lukich would never let him in. Most likely, he was sneaking in through the attic window—I could tell he knew that passage well. Which meant he had to climb the roof, crossing over from the neighbor's house. What made him do that? Could it be that Falcon House was a place to hide from his brutal master?

Vanyousha's master—oh, how I loathed him! What monster would hurt a little boy? And for what? For his not drawing silly pictures? I vowed to myself that when I encountered Vanyousha's master, I'd challenge him to a duel with rapiers and kill him.

For an instant, I fancied that my pen was a rapier. I drove it into the paper so hard, the nib split open. I pulled the broken pieces out of the grip, tossed them on the floor, and searched the drawers of the desk for a replacement. By turns, I slid the drawers open, all gray with dust and shaped like little coffins, wider at the front and narrower at the end. Aside from a few withered flies, all of the drawers were empty. I nearly missed the last drawer—a wide and shallow tray below the top of the desk. I opened it. Something black, thick at one end and thin at the other,

Дедушкинъ кнутъ

lay under the coat of dust. It was a horsewhip. I shuddered, recalling Vanyousha's lacerated back.

Oh, how I wished my grandfather were still alive! He was a fearless rider and had this horsewhip always by his side, just as Shysh said. He would have known how to protect Vanyousha. He would have given the monster who had whipped Vanyousha a taste of it himself!

I pulled the whip out of the drawer. The braided leather grip felt good. I shook it twice to untangle the lash, stood up, and raised the whip. I spun the lash, slowly at first, then faster until it whooshed above my head in circles. Then I plunged it forward and snapped it back. The crack shattered the silence of the chamber. The lash flickered by the covered portrait, and when it snatched the bedsheet off its frame, Grandfather seemed to smile at me in approval.

CHAPTER FORTY-THREE

In which Prince Lev and his grandfather
appear side by side in the mirror

Someone knocked, the door cracked open, and Woldemar
peeked in. "Excuse me for interrupting, Your Excellency,"
he said in an undertone, eyeing the horsewhip in my hand
with alarm. "Madam sent a garment for Your Excellency
to wear to dinner."

His head disappeared. Behind the door, two hushed
voices began arguing, something fell, and Woldemar's voice
hissed angrily, "Pick it up!" The door flew open, and the

tailor from the mothball cellar was pushed into the room. Clutching to his chest a pair of boots and an army uniform fastened to a hanger, he glared wildly at the chamber and tried to force his way back out, but Woldemar blocked the door. Without hesitation, the tailor head-butted him in the belly. Woldemar gasped and kicked the tailor on the shin. The tailor cried out in pain and, dropping the boots and the uniform to the floor, began hopping around on one leg.

"Stop this at once!" I cried. "What are you two doing?"

The tailor froze on one leg like a stork and gaped at me with a terrified expression.

"This is the tailor who will help Your Excellency with the garment," said Woldemar, and, snatching the boots and the uniform off the floor, thrust them into the tailor's hands. The tailor, wobbling on one leg, managed to keep standing, but he dropped the boots. He leaned over and picked up the boots but dropped the uniform. He picked up the uniform but dropped the boots. And he kept picking up the one while dropping the other until I got there to rescue him.

"Enough of this circus!" I said, gathering the boots off the floor and catching the falling uniform. The tailor, the boots, and the uniform stunk of mothballs. "What is your name?"

"Maurice, Your Excellency." The tailor bowed. "Madam's costumier."

"Costumier!" snorted Woldemar. "Quit blabbering!" He flung a worried glance at me. "Your Excellency must get dressed. Madam's guest is expected any minute."

Maurice cautiously followed me to the mirror, looking about uneasily. Trying not to make any noise, he set the boots down beside the mirror and carefully spread the uniform upon the sofa. It was the gold-braided crimson outfit I'd seen him altering in the cellar.

Woldemar remained in the doorway, watching the tailor fuss over me. The moment Maurice began squeezing me into the uniform, his fear of the chamber seemed to vanish. With his teeth clenching pins, he circled me swiftly, tightening something in one place, and then tightening something in another. Slashing me with chalk and sticking me with pins, he suddenly ripped a stand-up collar off the tunic, and in a flash reattached it again, but so tightly he placed it round my neck, the collar nearly strangled me. At last, he set a shiny helmet over my head, very heavy because the Imperial double-headed eagle made of brass sat on top of it. Then he took a step back, cocked his head, and, with one eye tightly shut, he looked me up and down.

"A perfect fit!" he announced, and, with a glance at Woldemar, added, "Why don't you come in and take a look?"

"I can see from here. Fits you like a glove, Your Excellency."

Indeed, the uniform fit marvelously. The tunic was skintight and the trousers, also close-fitting, were tucked into tall riding boots polished like mirrors. I smiled, recalling the silly disguise that Vanyousha had worn in the cellar.

Я съ дедушкой въ зеркалѣ

With a proud smile, Maurice took off his glasses, rubbed them on the front of his waistcoat, and set them back on his nose. Suddenly he paled and, pointing at the mirror with his trembling finger, stammered, "Lord, have mercy . . . Your Excellency is the very picture of—"

The doubled reflection he was pointing at was startling. Grandfather's portrait was hanging in the shadowy recess behind my back, so that he appeared to be standing alongside me in the mirror. Of course, I was much younger than he was in the portrait, but painted in exactly the same uniform I now wore, the resemblance between us was striking.

CHAPTER FORTY-FOUR

In which Prince Lev delights his ancestors

Olga Lvovna did not reveal whom I was to meet tonight, but judging by the transformation of the house, she was expecting an important guest. The rooms that had seemed so frightening in the night but pitiful by daylight now looked magnificent. They had been thoroughly cleaned and flooded with brilliant light, the dusty slipcovers removed to reveal lavish furnishings, and beneath my boots, floors shone like mirrors. As we passed from room to room, the eyes of the red-liveried servants, flanking every doorway with their lighted candelabrums, followed me in awe.

"May God give you good health," whispered one servant behind me.

"And the rank of general," whispered another.

I clenched my teeth for fear that I might reveal my feelings with a silly grin and, without a glance at them, continued walking. Woldemar smiled and, leaning over my ear, whispered, "You look splendid in your grandfather's garment, Your Excellency."

We were just passing a mirror, and I couldn't help but peek at my reflection. Where was that puny shape bundled up in scarves and plastered with snow that had gazed back at me from the mirror upon my arrival? That cowed boy was gone forever. Bound now in my grandfather's crimson and gold, my back was straighter, my step was firmer, and my head held higher.

Followed by Woldemar, I marched through the salon where the well-polished death masks of my ancestors gleamed in the dazzling candlelight. As before, I felt their gaze, but now they were watching me with pride. *Here comes the master of the house*, they seemed to say, *a hero, a decorated general—Prince Lev, whose own death mask will join us on these sacred walls one splendid day.*

The thought of my own death mask made me feel a little uneasy. Every time I felt uneasy in Falcon House, which was more often than I would have liked, I thought of Mother. I thought of her now.

If only Mother could've seen me in my grandfather's uniform, how happy she would have been, and happier still if she had known that soon she would be joining me here. True, I wasn't quite the master of this house yet, but I already looked like one. Besides, I had no choice; I must become its master—I was the only twig left on our family tree.

"Stairs are this way, Your Excellency," said Woldemar, and with a little sly smile added, "The elevator is out of order."

CHAPTER FORTY-FIVE

In which Prince Lev confronts a Cossack

Marching up the well-lighted stairs, I listened with pleasure to the spurs jingling at the heels of my riding boots and regretted not bringing Grandfather's horsewhip with me. Grandfather was a fearless rider and had always carried the horsewhip, and though I'd never ridden a horse, the sound of my jingling spurs made me imagine that one day I would be a fearless rider too. I must order the coachman Klim to bring me the chestnut mare that had carried me here from the railway station. That mare was fast, but under my whip it would fly. Clad in my grandfather's uniform, I would ride it at full gallop up and down Saint Petersburg so everyone could see me. I was just thinking how the passersby would stop in their tracks to admire me when someone barked, "Who goes there?"

A giant man with a turned-up mustache and a beard parted in the middle stepped from round the corner and looked severely at me. He was one of those Cossacks everyone was always so scared of. The Cossacks were wild and very good with swords and pistols.[13]

"This is Madam Lvov's nephew, officer," timidly replied Woldemar.

The Cossack glared at me with suspicion. "Nephew, eh?" He twisted the ends of a mustache black as coal. "What's his name?"

The top of my head reached to about the handle of the dagger at the Cossack's belt. I should have been scared of him like everybody else, but somehow, clad in my

Казакъ и на Лунѣ.

grandfather's uniform, I wasn't. Besides, in my fancy, I was still astride my chestnut mare, and so instead of the Cossack looking at me from above, it was *I* looking down at him.

"I am Prince Lvov, the master of this house," I said in a firm voice. "I mean, the future master," I added quickly.

The Cossack glanced at Woldemar, who nodded gravely, then squinted back at me. I stomped my boot impatiently. "I am expected!" I cried. "Step out of the way at once!" The jingle of my spur echoed sharply up and down the stairs.

The Cossack blinked and held two fingers to his hat. "Beg your pardon, Your Excellency." He clicked his heels. "My mistake. This way, please."

I gave him a quick nod in a military manner and, as I was marching up the stairs, heard Woldemar dashing after me.

The house teemed with Cossacks, peering at us from behind every corner. The nearer we came to the dining salon, the more Cossacks there were, all armed to the teeth.

But word that the future master of Falcon House was on his way must have reached them, for not one dared to stop us again.

The double doors to the dining salon were guarded by dozens of Cossacks, taller, broader, and more heavily armed than the others. When we approached, they silently parted, and one of them bent at the waist to hold open the door for me.

CHAPTER FORTY-SIX

*In which Prince Lev meets
Olga Lvovna's guest*

As soon as I entered the brilliantly lighted salon, I noticed the solemn expressions the servants wore on their faces. Lined up at attention along an enormous table set with crystal and porcelain gleaming atop a snow-white cloth, they eyed a large, bearded man pleasantly chatting with Olga Lvovna. When the door closed softly behind me, the two ceased talking and looked at me.

"Our hero at last!" Olga Lvovna exclaimed, and, leaning toward the man, added in a theatrical whisper, "He was in a dreadful accident today. The lift fell and was smashed to smithereens, but by the grace of God, the child survived."

The man nodded and looked at me with curiosity. He looked oddly familiar. I knew I had seen him before, but when and where I couldn't recall. As I approached, I even began to have a peculiar notion that once I had drawn his likeness in my album.

"Please allow me to introduce Prince Lev," said Olga Lvovna. "Excellent breeding, grace, and charm inherited from his grandfather. May he kiss your hand?"

The man gave a gracious smile and stuck his hand in my face. The hand was thick and smelled of soap, the fingernails were trimmed and neatly filed, and on the plumpish pinky, a ring sparkled with a double-headed eagle set in diamonds.

I peered at the hand in silence.

"Kiss it, kiss it," hissed Olga Lvovna. "His Majesty is waiting!"

I turned cold, then hot, then cold again. Before me

Александръ 3ий

stood His Imperial Majesty Alexander III, the Tsar of Russia,[14] and I had failed to recognize him. He kept smiling and holding out his hand for me to kiss, but I was so struck with shame, I simply couldn't move. An awkward silence followed.

"The child is still in shock from the accident, Your Majesty," remarked Olga Lvovna, giving me a steely look.

"Never mind, never mind," said the emperor, lowering his hand. "Once I was a shy youth myself." His beady eyes scrutinized me. "A remarkable likeness, however, a double of his grandfather. Even the outfit!"

The emperor's fleshy nose twitched. Abruptly he leaned in and sniffed at my tunic. "What's that peculiar smell, my boy?" he whispered, glancing at me in alarm. "Mothballs?" He moved away a little.

I stood as if nailed down, powerless to move or speak. The emperor exchanged glances with Olga Lvovna and then both looked back at me. Nobody spoke. The emperor folded his hands behind his back and, fixing me with his beady eyes, began rocking to and fro from his heels to his toes, his boots squeaking as he rocked. I stared at him without blinking.

After a while, a clock chimed somewhere in the house. The emporer cleared his throat and said, "So, my boy, the princess tells me you're dreaming of entering the Corps des Pages?"

I couldn't answer. I still could not utter a word.

He glanced at Olga Lvovna and continued, "Admirable, my boy, admirable. I was once a dreamer myself, as all boys are, I suppose. What are your interests?"

"Prince is a remarkable artist," put in Olga Lvovna. "His portrait of me is unlike anything you might witness in art, Your Majesty."

"Art could be useful," the emperor said. "But I must warn you, my boy—too much of it could lead to a man's undoing. Take your grandfather, for example. Are you familiar with his demise?"

Olga Lvovna's eyes shot to me in alarm. "The child has a high-strung nature, Your Majesty. Perhaps—"

"What nature?" he said.

"High-strung, Your Majesty. Perhaps after the accident I mentioned, it might be too disturbing for him to hear—"

"Women's talk, my dear." The emperor waved his hand dismissively, and the diamond eagle on his pinky flashed. "To be admitted to the Corps des Pages, the boy must learn to face truth like a man. Besides"—he chuckled—"the story is terribly amusing."

Olga Lvovna opened her mouth to object but bit her tongue. The emperor noticed, nodded in approval, and, combing with both hands his black, glistening beard, began telling his story.

CHAPTER FORTY-SEVEN

In which the emperor tells his amusing story

"As you may know, my boy, your grandfather was a passionate hunter. He kept an enormous hunt, best in Russia. Falcons, hounds, huntsmen, you name it—a regular army. Once, traveling the countryside with his hunting party, he comes upon a village where the preparation for a flogging is in progress. A young serf is to be flogged. Your grandfather decides to view the affair and is invited. The tea is served. Your grandfather asks what the boy has done.

'Instead of working, the boy draws pictures,' comes the answer. 'The wretch thinks himself an artist.'

"Keenly interested, your grandfather demands to view the wretch's pictures. The pictures are brought in. Naturally, the pictures are sheer nonsense: the boy's mother at a samovar, some old peasant with dirty spoons, a babe playing with a kitty on a filthy floor. Ridiculous, of course, but your grandfather, who was forever trying to impress my father with silly novelties . . ." The emperor lifted his eyes to the ceiling and chuckled. "To impress my father? Ha-ha. As though such a thing were possible."

He gazed back at me and continued, "The little serf who draws is certainly a novelty, so your grandfather decides to buy the boy and bring him to our palace. 'Name any price,' he says to the master of the boy. The master, a local landowner fond of falconry, points to your grandfather's favorite falcon, Milka, and offers an exchange. 'Give me the bird and have your boy,' he says, 'and I will throw in his mother for good measure.' "

The emperor glanced at Olga Lvovna. "Do you recall Milka, Princess?"

"How can I forget, Your Majesty? That nasty bird would screech its head off every time I tried to dance for Daddy." She paused and added gloomily, "That always made him laugh."

The emperor gave a chuckle and went on. "Yes, my boy, your grandfather loved her. The bird, I mean. So should he give up his falcon and get the boy? He can't decide. He is in agony. Yet his desire to impress the emperor prevails, and he returns to Petersburg without Milka but with the grubby little serf—"

"What about the boy's mother?" I said.

"What mother?" The emperor frowned. "The boy's mother has nothing to do with the story."

"But still," I insisted. "Did she come with him?"

"No, no," the emperor said, annoyed. "His mother was left on your grandfather's estate somewhere, in some village. It's irrelevant."

Suddenly Olga Lvovna clapped her hands and said cheerfully, "Well, perhaps we should have dinner."

"I'm not finished, my dear," the emperor said sternly. "I'm just getting to the juicy part."

"Please continue, Your Majesty," she said with a sigh. "You always narrate this story with such feeling."

"In Petersburg," the emperor went on, "your grandfather takes the boy into society in order to test his skills. The serf surprises everyone with an amusing gift of which your grandfather was not aware. Besides those pathetic peasants, samovars, and kitties, the serf is capable of drawing anything you ask of him, anything at all—things he could never have seen or even heard of. Overnight, he becomes a Petersburg sensation. Next, your grandfather, much excited, delivers the boy to our palace. The easel is set, paper, pens, ink. Everything is ready. The entire court is present. We enter: Father, Mother, and all of us kids. I'm holding Mama's hand. We sit down. Your grandfather, with a proud smile, bids his serf to draw. Nothing doing. We're waiting, but the boy stands stupefied, neither dead nor quite alive. A minute passes, two, three. A nasty smell reaches our nostrils. Lo and behold, the boy has wet his pants from fright!"

The emperor snorted, slapped his knee, and burst out laughing. "Hilarious, my boy! Hilarious! You should have seen your poor grandfather's face! Ha! Ha! Ha!"

"What happened after?" I asked cautiously.

"What?" the emperor said, laughing so hard, his eyes were moist with tears. "Why, nothing. Your grandfather took the boy away and had his servants flog him. What else?"

"What else?" I echoed. "What happened to the boy?"

The emperor's large stomach still shook from laughter when he replied, "The boy died under the whip."

I noticed that Olga Lvovna was watching me intently. Our eyes locked for an instant, and something like a spark passed from her eyes into mine. I blinked. She looked away.

"Remarkable memory, Your Majesty," she said. "You were still a child then."

"Oh yes, yes, that was long ago, before Father freed the serfs. Some say, my boy, your grandfather is to blame for the emancipation of the serfs. My father was so dismayed that the artistic serf boy expired during the flogging, he made haste to sign the Emancipation Manifesto."[5]

"What was the boy's name?" I said quietly.

The emperor lifted his eyes to the ceiling and combed his beard. "Let me think . . . His name was . . . Oh, yes, your grandfather called him Vanyousha."

Suddenly, with a terrific bang, a gust of wind blasted a window open behind the emperor. The candles flared and went out, and in the flooded moonlight, the window drapes rose, flapping heavily.

"Guards!" the emperor screamed. "Guards!"[6]

The door flew open and in burst the Cossacks. I was swept aside. There was a loud crack and a flash in the dark. Someone fired a pistol. Olga Lvovna screamed. The Cossacks, fumbling with their daggers, circled the emperor. In the moonlight, the whites of their rolling eyes and the gleaming blades of their daggers stood out sharply.

By the window, the servants were snatching at the banging frame. The wind hurled snowflakes into the room, and something made of glass rolled off the table, fell to the floor, and broke.

At last, the window was shut, candles brought, and when the room was bright once more, blue smoke stood layered in the air. It smelled like gunpowder.

"Thank you for the enchanting evening, Princess," said the emperor as his eyes darted around the room uneasily. "But I must run."

"Already?" Olga Lvovna thrust out her lower lip like a sulking child. "You haven't eaten yet, Your Majesty."

"Next time, Princess, next time. As your father used to say, duties before everything."

"How true, Your Majesty," Olga Lvovna said, and lowered her eyes. "Thank you for visiting a pathetic and abandoned invalid."

"We'll have none of that, my dear!" The emperor shook his thick finger at Olga Lvovna. "We'll see you dancing yet."

He dashed toward the exit, but, catching sight of me, he halted. "Ah! Yes! The boy." He stepped up to me swiftly and put his pudgy hand upon my shoulder. "I will have a word with the director of the Corps des Pages about you, my boy. If your spirit is as equal to your grandfather's as your looks are, I trust they shall permit you to join without entry exams. I always said examinations were silly business. I'd never have passed them! Ha-ha-ha!"

Encircled by the Cossacks bristling with daggers, the emperor fled the room.

CHAPTER FORTY-EIGHT

In which Prince Lev is spoon-fed by his aunt

When the stomping of the Cossacks' boots receded behind the closed door, strained silence settled in the room. Olga Lvovna sat stiffly in her wheelchair and the servants stood in their places, but now their eyes were fastened not on the emperor as before but on me. I felt their scrutiny but did not look up, pretending to be deep in thought. The door creaked open, and all eyes strayed to Woldemar, who slipped into the room and, stepping noiselessly, approached Olga Lvovna.

"Shall the men clear the table, madam?" he whispered.

"What for?" snapped Olga Lvovna. "Are you trying to starve me to death? Prince and I will eat."

"I'm not hungry."

"Nonsense. Push me to the table, Woldemar. Prince, sit near me. Let us be cozy."

Woldemar steered Olga Lvovna's chair to the table, and obediently I followed. The servant moved my chair out, I lowered into my seat, and, as he moved the chair back in, another servant swiftly tucked the napkin behind my collar. The napkin was so stiffly starched it nearly cut my throat. The soup bowl emblazoned with our family's coat of arms was set before me. The soup was brought. While a white-gloved servant silently ladled the soup into my bowl, I watched our coat of arms disappear beneath the steaming liquid.

"Why don't you eat, Prince?" inquired Olga Lvovna.

Why didn't I eat? Perhaps because the story I had just heard made me so weary, there was no strength left in me to even lift the spoon.

Княжна Ольга Львовна

Olga Lvovna sighed deeply and, leaning closer, filled my spoon with soup. She blew on it to cool the steaming liquid and gently brought the spoon to my lips. I swallowed a spoonful. The soup was delicious. I swallowed another spoonful and then another. She spoon-fed me until the bowl was empty. I glanced at her out of the corner of my eye. She smiled, then glared angrily at Woldemar. "Don't you feed him, villain? The child is wasting away like a candle!"

The second course was roasted goose. With a solemn air, a servant drove a fork into the goose and carved it. Olga Lvovna ordered him to fill my plate and generously spooned applesauce and gravy on top of it herself. She wanted to continue feeding me and seemed disappointed when I declined politely. All at once I realized just how ravenous I was. Aside from those cream puffs, I hadn't eaten since I had come to Petersburg.

Watching me devour the goose, Olga Lvovna shook her head and, after a long and mournful sigh, remarked, "I know, my dear boy, just how troubled you must feel right now. No sooner do you meet a boy named . . . what was it?"

"Vanyousha," prompted Woldemar.

"A boy named Vanyousha, flogged apparently by someone, than here comes His Majesty with that tale about a boy also named Vanyousha and also flogged but . . . years and years ago. Coincidence? I doubt it." Her face assumed a compassionate expression. "I fear you have encountered a ghost, my dear."

"The boy I met was not a ghost," I said, and tore off the goose leg with my fingers. "Vanyousha is a real boy."

"A real boy?" she echoed in surprise.

"Yes," I replied, cramming the leg into my mouth. "I don't believe in ghosts."

Olga Lvovna and Woldemar exchanged astonished glances, but when she looked at me again, she was smiling. "You are becoming a real Lvov, my dear. No Lvov was ever—"

"Given to superstitions," I completed her phrase with my mouth full.

She laughed. "Then let us not mention it again, Prince. We'll speak of only pleasant things." She lifted the lorgnette to her eyes. "You look marvelous in your costume. A remarkable likeness to your grandfather, as His Majesty so keenly observed."

"I don't want to look like him anymore."

"Why not?"

"Because of what he did. That boy Vanyousha . . . that other boy . . . was murdered on his orders."

"If anyone is to blame, Prince, blame the boy," objected Olga Lvovna. "He drove your grandfather into an early grave."

"How could he do that?" I said, gnawing on a bone. "The boy died under the whip."

"Indeed," agreed Olga Lvovna, "but did this Vanyousha pass away as all respectable dead do? Oh no. He stayed on."

"What do you mean, stayed on?"

"He became a ghost."

The bone got stuck in my throat, and I began to choke.

"Breathe through your nose, Prince," said Olga Lvovna calmly.

I scraped my chair away from the table, tore off the napkin, and yanked at my collar. Just then, Olga Lvovna walloped my back with such force that the bone shot out of my throat like a bullet and splashed into my water glass. Instantly, a white-gloved servant replaced the glass.

"Better?" inquired Olga Lvovna.

"The boy became a ghost?" I wheezed, rubbing my throat.

"He did indeed," she replied. "In this very house." She glanced at my plate of mutilated goose. "The next course is fish, Prince. Sturgeon. I'll tell them to debone it."

"I'm not hungry anymore," I said. "But . . . but what happened after he became a ghost?"

"The nasty imp tormented your grandfather in daylight and at night. Soon Daddy—how shall I put it?—became a little touched. He lost his mind. I mean, completely. On the very day the serfs were freed, he stabbed himself to death."

"He stabbed himself?"

"Yes, with a rapier. Playing musketeers with the ghost, I suppose."

To hide my panic, I brought the water glass to my lips. My teeth tapped so noisily against the glass, I had to set it back down.

"But that boy . . . that ghost . . . he left after my grandfather passed away?"

"To my never-ending sorrow," sighed Olga Lvovna, "he did not. The filthy brat stayed on to haunt my house. Unheard-of horrors take place daily. This afternoon down in the cellar, a set of clothes and a pair of boots attacked my men."

"He didn't attack them!" I blurted out.

Olga Lvovna raised her eyebrow. "Were you there?"

"No."

"Of course not." She scrutinized me coldly for a moment, then gave me an imploring look. "If only someone could uncover what that demon wants from us, my dear Prince. After all, your grandfather departed long ago. Why is that boy still haunting us?"

There was a pause. All eyes were on me.

"You look a little pale, Prince. Did I frighten you? Perhaps you'd like to sleep elsewhere tonight?"

I thought about it. "No," I said.

"As you wish, my dear." She made a sign to Woldemar. "Take me to my rooms. I am exhausted."

I stood up as Woldemar steered Olga Lvovna's chair out of the room.

"Aunt!"

They halted in the doorway. "Yes, Prince?"

"What if . . . what if that boy Vanyousha never left because he believes that he is not free to go?"

"How do you mean?"

"What if he doesn't know that the serfs were given freedom? He believes that he must still draw pictures for Grandfather."

"Ridiculous! The boy can't draw pictures. He is dead."

"But what if he was waiting for someone to help him draw those pictures?"

A faint smile appeared on her lips. "I wonder who that might be?"

"I don't know. Someone who could help him to join his mother."

"It is sheer nonsense, Prince. He'd sooner join her if he moved on to hell, where imps like him and their mothers go. Good night, Prince."

Just as Woldemar wheeled the chair over the threshold, Olga Lvovna whacked him on the knee with her lorgnette. "Stop, villain!" He halted, and Olga Lvovna swung round to face me. "And if the fool cannot see that, Prince, someone must inform him that his mother is long dead. Dead, you hear?"

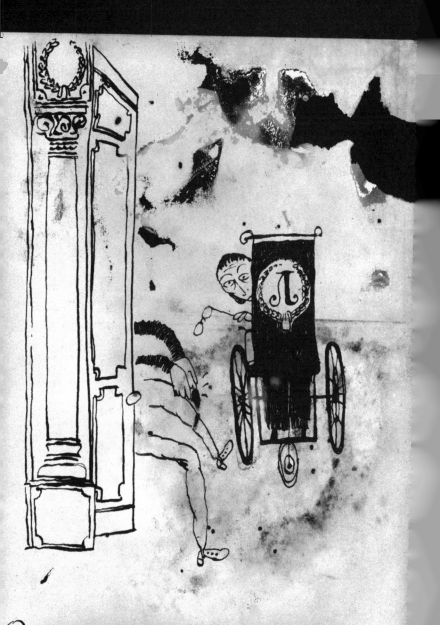

Ольга Львовна и бедный Вальдемаръ

CHAPTER FORTY-NINE

*In which Prince Lev completes the
drawing of his grandfather's chamber*

I slipped into the room, quietly closed the door behind me, and peered into the gloom at the edges of my grandfather's chamber.

"Come out, Vanyousha," I whispered. "I know everything."

The candle flames flared from the sound of my voice, but the chamber held its grave-like silence. From the uncovered portrait, Grandfather stared out of his painted eyes, and in the mirror across the room, his stare was repeated. I shuddered, caught between two pairs of eyes that seemed to burn right through me, but I made myself hold the stare. Had I looked away, I would have missed a sheet of paper lying on the floor that I could only see reflected in the mirror—the chair made of antlers obscured it from my position at the door. The paper lay beside the fireplace, whose throbbing light in turns illuminated the paper or concealed it under a leaping shadow. I couldn't look away from that scrap of paper, as if some unknown force riveted my sight to it. Without knowing what precisely, I knew that I had to do something to that sheet of paper. Something I had left unfinished.

Reluctantly, I stepped into the room. When I reached the chair made of antlers and knelt beside it to lift the paper off the floor, I had an uncanny feeling that the spikes were about to plunge into my hand. I snatched the paper, leaped back, and glared at the chair with suspicion. It stood as rigid as any chair.

I brought the paper to the desk and sat behind it. I suppose I'd known all along what was on that paper. The same confused perspective, uncertain contours, odd shapes, and, hideously slanted, a shadow of a human figure. It was the drawing of the chamber I had begun last night, continued sketching in my sleep, but had left unfinished.

I moved the candlestick a little closer, took the pen, blackened its nib in the inkwell, and held the pen over the sketch, uncertain how to proceed, or even whether I should proceed.

The candle flickered. The pen's shadow pulsated upon the drawing. A bead of ink, glistening below the nib, swelled slowly to a larger droplet, broke off, and fell. Inexplicably, I watched the droplet tumble for the longest time, observing in exact detail the way it stretched and shrunk before it hit the paper. When the droplet burst in total silence, the candle flared, and I felt an odd sensation in my arm, as if I had knocked my elbow against some solid object. My whole arm turned numb and tingled down to my fingertips. I could no longer feel the pen and wanted to let it go, but my fingers did not obey me. Instead, they gripped the pen so hard my knuckles drained of blood.

There was a jolt at my shoulder and then another at my elbow, and all at once my hand began to move. The pen screeched across the paper, making rapid marks. Repeatedly I tried to stop my hand from moving but couldn't. It was as if someone else's hand, invisible but firm, was forcing my pen to move.

Soon the nib ran dry and began to scratch and shred the paper. I felt a grasp round my upper arm and, in panic, saw my hand darting to the inkwell, blackening the nib, and darting back. I didn't know I was crying until my tears fell and mixed with ink over the mangled paper. Furiously the pen continued moving. I clenched my teeth and gripped my right hand with my left to halt the movement. At once, some uncanny force flung aside my left hand to prevent it from meddling. I tried to rise, but my legs had no strength. My whole body violently trembled. My hand continued moving. In the dead air of the room, the only sounds were of the scratching pen and of my sobs. Suddenly I heard a scream. It was horrifying! For an instant I couldn't understand who was screaming, but then I understood that it was I. My hand tossed the pen aside, rose above my head, and came down hard, smashing its knuckles against the drawing. My screaming ceased.

Panting, I sat gazing at my hand. Now at rest, it lay palm up, fingers trembling lightly. I tried to move my arm, and it obediently followed. The spell was over.[17]

CHAPTER FIFTY

*In which Prince Lev learns the truth
about his grandfather*

The drawing of Grandfather's chamber lay before me. It was finally complete. My own hand had made this drawing, but it was Vanyousha who had moved my hand. There was no doubt of this now. By what sorcery had he accomplished this? He had told me that his own hand had become clumsy, that nothing stuck to paper. That was why he had wanted me to draw his mama drinking tea, his uncle with wooden spoons, a tiny babe playing with a kitty. He had wanted me to draw sweet pictures so he could join his mama in the village. But I never did. Instead, I drew pictures for *my* mother. Surprised that I could draw so well, I had chosen not to question my sudden gift. Could it be that, out of the kindness of his heart, Vanyousha had helped me to draw my pictures so that I could join *my* mother—even if he couldn't join *his?*

Mother told me, "Don't simply follow the rules. Draw from your heart, Levushka." The pictures that I'd drawn since coming to Falcon House had stemmed not from my heart but from Vanyousha's. At last, I understood what Mother had tried to teach me. Instead of following Grandfather's cruel rules, she wanted me to draw out of the kindness of my heart, much the way Vanyousha could.

I felt that someone's eyes were watching me, and quickly I looked up.

"Vanyousha?"

From the portrait, my grandfather stared at me. His gaze filled me not with fear as before, but with an oppressive feeling. I had profited from Vanyousha's gift, just as he had. Grandfather had wanted to impress the emperor, and I had wanted to impress my mother. We both let Vanyousha's kindly heart and talent do the work for us. My aunt insisted that I become like Grandfather. Did I satisfy her wishes? Was I like him now?

Looking at the drawing my hand had just completed, I knew that it was my grandfather—not some servants on his orders, but he himself, a noble hero with a heart of gold, according to my aunt—who had flogged that little boy to death. My grandfather, in whose footsteps I had tried so hard to follow, was a murderer.

The instrument that had killed Vanyousha, my grandfather's horsewhip, lay coiled beside me. Fighting nausea, I reached for its braided handle. The handle felt warm, as if only moments before it had been in the grip of the murderer's hand.

CHAPTER FIFTY-ONE

In which Prince Lev sets Vanyousha free

The air vibrated. There was a patter of bare feet, the candles flared, light darted up the wall, and in the brief glare between two moving shadows, I saw Vanyousha. He was exactly as he had come to me last night, pitiful and frightened. When our eyes met, he gasped and cried, falling to his knees, "Don't hurt me, spirit! Have mercy!" His voice quivered and he burst out crying. "Holy Mother of God, Father, Son, and Holy Ghost!" He clasped his hands and rolled his white-lashed eyes. "Our help and our aid in distress, deliver me from this wicked spirit that besets me . . ."

I rose from my chair and walked slowly to him. In the silence of the room, the jangling of my spurs, which only just a while ago had made me so proud, now sickened me. As I knelt beside Vanyousha, he cried and raised his hands, as if to guard his face against a coming blow.

"Don't hurt me!"

"It's me, Vanyousha," I said, surprised. "Don't you recognize me?"

His eyes flickered over my uniform. "Master?" he whispered. "Forgive me, master."

"Forgive you? For what, Vanyousha?"

"I was just scared, master. Please take me back."

"I don't understand, Vanyousha. Take you where?"

"Take me to the Tsar. I'll do right this time. I'll draw, I promise." His eyes shifted off my face and fixed upon my hand. "Please don't beat me, master."

I followed his gaze—my hand still gripped the horsewhip. In disgust, I tossed the thing aside, and when it thumped against the floor, Vanyousha's eyes rolled in their sockets. He collapsed, violently shaking. I spun round in panic. I had to do something! I had to help Vanyousha, but how? The reflection I caught in the mirror repulsed me. No wonder Vanyousha mistook me for his master; in his gold-and-crimson uniform, I was Grandfather's living image. Instinctively, my eyes shifted to his portrait. Grandfather's eyes beamed out of his face like blazing lights. The artist's trick by which I had cleverly explained away his living eyes was useless now. His eyes still glared, but not at me. Full of menace, his eyes glared at Vanyousha.

Pitiful, animal-like moans came from the poor boy. I turned away from the portrait and leaned over Vanyousha. All at once, I knew what I must do.

"Listen to your master now," I said in a grown-up voice. "Listen carefully."

He opened his eyes and, trembling, gazed at me.

"You do not have to draw any more pictures for me, Vanyousha. I grant you freedom. Go back to your village. Go back to your mama. You are free, Vanyousha."

"Free?" he echoed with a sob.

"Free," I said. "Your troubles are over."

A sweet smile appeared on his quivering lips. Something lit up in his luminous eyes, and at once he was transformed. His face was made beautiful and flooded with light. Holding my breath, I watched that light slowly fade and become translucent, and with it the whole of Vanyousha became translucent as well. The shooting star that Vanyousha and I had watched from the roof of the house had faded in the same way Vanyousha faded now— slowly, gently, and silently.

I remained still for another moment, then rose quickly and strode to where I had dropped the rapier with which I had so carelessly cowed Vanyousha. I had made a promise to myself that when I encountered Vanyousha's master, I'd challenge him to a duel with rapiers and I would kill him. The best I could do now was to seize the rapier off the floor and rush at Grandfather's portrait. I slashed the canvas into two long, cross-shaped gashes.

A growing rumble rolled through the chamber, a ripple

billowed through the walls. They heaved, as if inhaling the dreadful air in this room. Flames in the fireplace roared and, for an instant, the room was flooded with blinding brilliance. As the glow faded, the walls began to shrivel. In the dying light, I saw the chamber for what it really was—decrepit and decayed and furry with mold. The warped, worm-eaten floor crumbled beneath my feet as I walked out.

CHAPTER FIFTY-TWO

In which Prince Lev remembers
what happened to his mother

There were faint whisperings in the dark. I heard glass clink against glass, a splash of water, and then something cool wet my brow. At certain hours, a quartered square began to glow behind my closed lids. I guessed it was a window. Against that hazy glow, someone's figure moved, sighing. I decided that it was Mother, called to Petersburg at last. I was recuperating from some unpleasant illness, and she was watching over me.

Once, Vanyousha came to visit. He sat timidly beside

my bed. He was a little scared of my mother. His huge, gray eyes followed her round the room and shot away each time she turned. I teased him and joked with Mother. We laughed, but when I looked again, Vanyousha was no longer there. He liked to vanish suddenly like that, then reappear someplace else, but this time he was gone for good. I looked for Mother, but she was gone as well.

In Vanyousha's place, my suit hung over the chair's back. Why did my aunt say the suit was gloomy? Because it was black? But it had to be black, it being a mourning suit. I wore it to the funeral I had to attend before I left for Petersburg.

The funeral had been brief; it was too cold. The grave-yard, gone white with snow, was riddled with crooked crosses and wreaths of rusted tin. In the silence, snowflakes were falling thickly against a marble tombstone. Before the tombstone gaped an open grave, and, next to it, two spades impaled a snowdrift. Abruptly, the silence was shattered by the gunfire of pounding hammers. When it stopped, four men in black trudged across the snow,

carrying a closed coffin. They lowered it into the grave, and two of them took up the spades. Below the ground, frozen lumps of earth clobbered the coffin's lid. The wind blew sharply, and when it swept aside the snowflakes shrouding the tombstone, I saw my mother's name carved into the marble.

CHAPTER FIFTY-THREE

In which Shysh serves his new master

"Owing to my experience in matters of etiquette," a voice squawked over me, "Madam has appointed me as Your Excellency's valet."

A warm cloth wiped crust from the corners of my eyes.

"Three days and three nights Your Excellency was pleased to repose. Madam ordered me to wake you."

I pushed the cloth away and, blinking, saw Shysh standing over me in a modest room filled with sunlight.

"Is it really true that Olga Lvovna appointed you to serve me?"

"Whom else would she appoint?" replied the offended valet. "After we found Your Excellency senseless on the stairs . . . You were pleased to swoon, Your Excellency, but no harm was done, thank heavens . . . Madam entrusted Your Excellency into my care. Will you take your breakfast now?"

"Raw meat again?"

"Why meat, Your Excellency?" Shysh crimsoned. "A proper breakfast."

He hobbled to the door. The door cracked open, someone giggled behind it, and through the opening a tray was thrust into the old man's hands. He brought the tray to me, halted, and looked me over critically.

"Your Excellency will be pleased to wash up first?"

"Eat first."

I leaned in and snatched the tray out of his hands. A plate of boiled eggs, a glass of steaming milk, and a stack of pancakes doused with honey covered the same tray that had twice before been brought to me.

"Grab a seat, Shysh," I said, fitting the tray into my lap. "I'm starving. This won't take long."

He glared at me, aghast. "That'd be against the rules, Your Excellency. Master would've—"

"I am your master now, Shysh. Sit down."

Shysh looked about him uneasily, found a chair, and, lifting his coattails, perched at the edge of the seat.

"Tell me, Shysh, did my grandfather ever flog you?"

He looked at me sideways without replying.

"Speak up, Shysh."

"Flogging was allowed then, Your Excellency. It was before our Tsar was pleased to free us."

"Did he flog you?"

"For my own good, he did."

"For your own good?"

He looked away and mumbled, as if embarrassed by his own words, "To be sure, Your Excellency. They were good old days."

"I tell you what, Shysh." I shoved a whole hard-boiled egg into my mouth. "Those days are over."

CHAPTER FIFTY-FOUR

In which Shysh tells of a ghastly episode

Shysh helped me wash and dress, combed my hair, sprinkled me with aromatic water, and, satisfied with my appearance, escorted me to Olga Lvovna's quarters.

As on the day of my arrival, servants crowded the doorways to watch me pass. But instead of gaping at me with curiosity, as if expecting some oddity from me, some rare trick, as if I were a circus bear, they looked at me with gratitude. Some bowed deeply, some blessed me as I passed, and some, older women mostly, held handkerchiefs to their eyes, shaking their heads and sighing.

Shysh hobbled beside me and, at intervals, shook his shriveled finger at the servants. "What's there to look at, people?" he squawked with the proudest grin. "Go back to your duties."

In the anteroom to Olga Lvovna's chamber, the picture of our family tree stood on the floor, leaning against the wall. The glass within the frame had shattered.

"What happened here?"

"The very night Your Excellency was pleased to have a fainting spell, a ghastly episode took place. The whole house shook as if the Devil himself were moving out. Many valuable objects were lost." His voice sunk to a whisper. "Your Excellency's ancestors' death masks were perfectly smashed."

At that moment, there was a sound of quick steps inside the chamber, the door flew open, and Woldemar appeared. "Right this way, Your Excellency," he said in an excited voice. "Madam's waiting."

CHAPTER FIFTY-FIVE

In which Olga Lvovna makes a confession

"Thank heavens, Prince, you have color in your cheeks," exclaimed Olga Lvovna as I entered her chamber. "The doctor who examined you assured me that you were not in danger, but still I was in anguish. Bring Prince a chair, Woldemar."

"I'd rather stand," I said, weary of her abusing Woldemar for choosing the wrong chair.

She smiled, as if she had guessed my thought. "Your noble breeding gave you such a pure heart, my dear."

Vanyousha had had a pure heart, but he was just a simple peasant boy. "Breeding has little to do with it, Aunt."

Her eyes flickered to Woldemar, then back to me. "Let us not go into that in front of the servants, Prince," she said, playfully shaking her bony finger at me. "Where is that chair, Woldemar?"

He brought a chair and set it beside the sofa on which Olga Lvovna was reclining. Before she could say a word, I plunked myself into the seat.

She gave a little laugh, leaned in to me, and whispered, "There's such lightness in my soul, I've no doubt we are no longer haunted." Unexpectedly, she winked at me. "I venture to suggest that you had something to do with it, my dear."

I opened my mouth to reply, but she interrupted me. "Don't breathe a word! I know what you will say. Your modesty is well known." She settled back into her pillows and heaved a sigh. "If you only knew, Prince, what I had to endure to rid Falcon House of its ghostly possession. For years I've been engaging experts in matters of the spectral world. Mediums, they call themselves, but they are mostly charlatans—and rather costly. I've had them here by the dozen. They'd sit around a table, holding hands and saying silly things." She closed her eyes and groaned in a ghostly voice, "Are you there, little boy? Speak to us, speak to us." She opened her eyes and laughed. "A useless bunch."[8]

"They were looking in the wrong place," I said. "It wasn't Vanyousha who haunted your house."

"How do you mean, Prince?"

"It was your father, Aunt. He was the one who wouldn't let Vanyousha go."

"I beg of you, my dear, do not speak poorly of Daddy. The man did what he could."

"You know *what* he did."

She started violently, flushed, and quickly looked away. "Woldemar?" she cried in a sudden fit of temper. "What have you done with my lorgnette?"

"It is next to you, madam."

"Don't mumble, villain. Where is it?"

"I do not mumble, madam," Woldemar replied. "I speak clearly."

Olga Lvovna gaped at him in astonishment, and as Woldemar did not look away in fear but remained with his eyes fixed calmly on her face, she shifted her gaze to me.

"I must congratulate you, Prince. These are the effects of your disrespect for our ancestors."

Glancing furiously at Woldemar, she reached toward the side table for her lorgnette. I followed the movement of her hand—the lorgnette was resting atop a stack of folded sheets of paper.

"But these are the pictures for my mother," I said, pointing at the stack. "You didn't send them."

The room was silent for a long and painful moment. Olga Lvovna gazed wearily at me. Her eyes lost their luster, and the corners of her straight-line mouth drooped slowly until her face resembled a death mask.

"I did not send your pictures, Prince" said she, "because there was no one to receive them. I believe you have known all along that your poor mother is dead."

I looked past Olga Lvovna. In the window behind her, a puffy cloud slowly unfurled against the cobalt sky.

"I am so sorry, Lev," Olga Lvovna said, and took my hand. "I am so, so sorry. As soon as I heard that you were orphaned, I sent for you."

I moved my hand away, and she winced as if from pain.

"From the telegram your governess sent," she continued, "I concluded that either you were ill from grief or that she was trying to deceive me for some purpose. But when you finally arrived, I knew that what she claimed was true."

"What did she say?"

"After you went to the funeral," said Olga Lvovna quietly, "after they took you home, you continued conversing with your mother, as though she were still alive. You saw your mother after she was buried." Her eyes welled up with tears. "You have been chosen for a cruel gift, Lev. You can see and hear the dead."

"Is that why you put me in Grandfather's study?" I

said after a pause, keeping my eyes on the window where the puffy cloud was drifting lazily above a snowy roof.

"I put you in Daddy's chamber so you could find that boy who haunted us. I used your gift to free Falcon House from possession."

She pulled out her handkerchief, covered her eyes, and sobbed. "You thought that I had summoned you to become the master of this house. In truth, I had sent my invitation because you had no one but me, Lev. I will provide for you while I am alive, and then Falcon House will be yours, but I beg you . . . forgive me, Lev. I took advantage of your gift."

I rose, collected my drawings, and, stepping to the door, glanced at the window, but by then the puffy cloud had dissolved without a trace.

CHAPTER FIFTY-SIX

*In which Prince Lev finishes the drawing
that couldn't be finished*

Spring came early. Every day, as if to celebrate the melting of the frozen river, church bells were ringing all over the city. To hear their music, I kept the window open, enjoying the sunshine and fresh air that poured into my room. At intervals, a light breeze leafed through the pages of the books spread on the windowsill, reminding me how much I still had to learn. His Majesty had promised that I could join the Corps des Pages without studying, but after Olga Lvovna admitted that my grandfather had been granted entry without passing his exams, I had chosen to decline the Royal favor.

I opened the Arithmetic, leafed through to the first set of problems, and embarked on solving them. Numbers had always troubled me a little, but I liked drawing their shapes. I drew a zero first, then went on to higher numerals. My pen screeched up and down, leaving marks on paper. How wonderful it was to draw. I used to love to sit beside my mother in our dining room and sketch together in my drawing album. Once, after nightfall, we were sketching Woolly. The cat was asleep, and now and then he would twitch his ears. Mother had sketched him from his tail, and I from his head, until our pens met over his tummy in the fold between the pages. How sweet it was to hear Woolly's measured breathing and beside me, Mother's voice humming softly. That was happiness.

Looking through my drawings, I found the sketch of Woolly. The sketch was of only half the cat; the other half would never be completed without Mother seated next to me. A beam of sunlight fell from the open window onto the drawing. I watched it move along the paper's creases and felt a soft, gentle wave passing through my arm. My fingers tingled faintly and closed tighter on the pen. The pen began to move. I watched it glide across the paper as it sketched Woolly's paws and fur and the stripes upon his tail. Fresh lines were moving toward the old ones. With bated breath, I heard the familiar voice humming as I watched my hand complete the picture.

Нашъ котъ Пушокъ

Это моя половинка

А это мамина

Winter 2015, Los Angeles, California.
The original pages of Prince Lvov's narrative
shortly before their final disintegration.

AFTERWORD

The completed drawing of the cat was the last surviving piece
of Prince Lev's narrative. Whether he passed his examinations to enter the boarding school and subsequently became
the master of Falcon House remains unknown. The pages that
I'd found years ago in my schoolyard disintegrated shortly
after I completed their translation, and no record of Lev's
subsequent life has been found.

According to the drawing of his family tree, Lev was born
in 1879 and still would have been a young man when the First
World War broke out. If he remained in Russia, it would have
taken a miracle for Lev to survive the calamities that followed the war. The Revolution of 1917 divided the nation
and resulted in civil war. Following that, the new Soviet
government initiated a reign of terror that lasted over thirty
years, under the leadership first of Vladimir Lenin and then

of Joseph Stalin. The famines of 1921, 1932, and 1947 took an enormous toll on the population. And, finally, the war with Nazi Germany from 1941 through 1945 claimed millions more lives. Regardless of when and where Prince Lev perished, he long ago joined the multitude of restless spirits that will forever haunt the history of Russia.

NOTES

1   The Lvovs were first mentioned in historical records during the reign of Ivan III in the second part of the fifteenth century. Then, in the eighteenth century, the line split into two branches. During the nineteenth century, both branches produced a great number of notable military commanders, cultural figures, and statesmen. After the Russian Revolution of 1917, the Russian aristocracy was severely persecuted by the new Bolshevik government. Some of the Lvovs fled Russia, while others remained. The Lvovs who emigrated survived. The Lvovs who remained behind were eventually annihilated, and their line terminated.

2   Saint Petersburg was founded in 1703 on the marshes along the Neva River by the emperor Peter the Great. During the construction of the city, the harsh working conditions and fierce climate claimed the lives of thousands of enslaved Russian peasants, or *serfs*. The city, the former capital of Russia, changed its name three times. In 1914, when Russia began fighting Germany in World War I, the German-sounding Saint Petersburg was changed to the Russian-sounding Petrograd. In 1924, after the death of the first leader of the new Communist state, Vladimir Ilyich Lenin, Petrograd was changed to Leningrad. In 1991, after the collapse of the Communist regime, Leningrad was changed back to Saint Petersburg. Whether Saint Petersburg will have other names remains to be seen, but presently the citizens of the city refer to it simply as Peter.

Today it is the second-largest city in Russia, an important cultural center, and a major port on the Baltic Sea.

3   Opulent eighteenth- and nineteenth-century mansions still line the streets of Saint Petersburg, but some were destroyed or completely transformed after the Russian Revolution of 1917. The exact address of Falcon House is unknown. However, Prince Lev's description of the city as viewed from the roof in Chapter Forty locates the mansion in proximity to the Neva River embankment. Most likely, Olga Lvovna resided either on Millionaires' Street, where members of the imperial family and those close to them had their residences, or on Morskaya Street, known as the "Golden Triangle" of Russian aristocracy.

4   A popular optical device in the nineteenth century, a *lorgnette* was a pair of magnifying lenses attached to a handle of varying length and material. Some handles were made of tortoiseshell, some of ivory, and some of metal, often ornate and studded with jewels. Prince Lev does not describe Olga Lvovna's lorgnette in detail, but apparently she used it not only to strengthen her vision but also to attack and intimidate her servants.

5   It appears that Olga Lvovna is prone to exaggeration. The first elevator in Saint Petersburg appeared in 1793 during the reign of Catherine II. Constructed by the famous inventor Ivan Kulibin, the elevator was installed in the Winter Palace, the residency of the Russian Tsars. Not until the 1870s did aristocratic homes such as Falcon House begin installing their own lifting machines.

6   Siberia is a vast Russian region to the east of the Ural Mountains known for its harsh climate. From the end of the sixteenth century until the second part of the twentieth, Siberia was used as a place of exile and forced labor for millions of political prisoners, prisoners of war, and common criminals.

7   Russian serfdom, a condition analogous to American slavery yet pecu-
    liar to Russia, was the forceful binding of peasants to land owned by
    nobles. The brutal servitude began in the Middle Ages and continued
    into the second part of the nineteenth century, constituting a funda-
    mental principle of Russia's social, political, and economic structure. By
    the time Tsar Alexander II finally abolished serfdom in 1861, over 22
    million peasants were in bondage to fewer than a hundred thousand
    landowners.

8   The first Russian translation of *The Three Musketeers*, a novel written by
    French author Alexandre Dumas, was published in Saint Petersburg in
    1846. Publisher Manukhin reprinted the book in 1866, and perhaps too
    that later edition Prince Lev is referring to. Dumas, who wrote his nov-
    els in installments for serial publications (his complete works fill 277
    volumes), was not a stickler for the historical facts, but the author could
    always be relied on to tell an exciting story.

9   Corps des Pages, Russia's most exclusive court and military academy,
    was founded in 1759 in order to train pages and officers of the Imperial
    Guards. Only those of noble descent and ancestral merit were admit-
    ted; however, the entrance examinations were extremely difficult. The
    academy produced a number of outstanding generals and statesmen
    over the years, until it was closed in 1917 as a result of the overthrow
    of the last Russian emperor, Nicholas II. The academy occupied the
    eighteenth-century Vorontsov Palace in Saint Petersburg on Sadovaya
    Street, number 26, only blocks away from where I lived with my family
    at number 68 and where, in my schoolyard, I came upon Prince Lev's
    papers.

10 Prince Lev's recollection of the operating method of the elevator leaves
    plenty of room for speculation as to what type of elevator it actually
    was. If we assume that the Lvovs' elevator was not the first in Saint

Petersburg, and therefore not the one designed by Ivan Kulibin based on the so-called screw-drive principal, then the elevator in Falcon House must have operated by either a hydraulic or an electric system. A hydraulic elevator required the digging of a well below the elevator's shaft. Given that Falcon House was a tall edifice, the well had to be very deep. However, in a city built upon marshes, such an operation would have been unsafe. Assuming that the elevator was electric, why then did candlelight and gas lamps light the rest of the house? It's possible that the financial status of the Lvovs by that time was so dismal that the wheelchair-bound Olga Lvovna was forced to direct all monies toward operating the elevator. This left no funds for covering the cost of illuminating a large mansion with electricity.

11 The earliest army uniforms that Prince Lev discovered in the cellar must have been fashioned after French and German military styles. Peter I, nicknamed the Great for his ambition, vigor, and foresight, not only reformed the Russian army according to the current European military science but also ordered his officers to shave off their traditional long beards and dress in the French clothing style. The first Russian monarch to receive education abroad, Peter came to be known for his drastic reforms, forcibly introducing the latest Western developments in science, art, and technology into Russian culture. While Peter's reforms allowed Russia to attain a status of one of the leading powers in Europe, many Russians still bemoan the loss of the unique cultural traditions that had existed prior to Peter's rule.

12 The Neva River depicted here by Prince Lev still flows through the very center of Saint Petersburg from Lake Ladoga into the Gulf of Finland. It is responsible for the city's high number of islands (100), canals (48), bridges (800), and embankments (over 100 miles). More than 300 floods have occurred in Saint Petersburg since its founding.

13 The original meaning of the word *Cossack* is "free man," for most of the Cossacks were runaway serfs. Having fled to sparsely populated areas in Southern Russia and Ukraine, Cossacks formed self-governing communities. The Russian government, fearing the Cossacks' daunting military skills, granted them special privileges and autonomy. In return, the Cossacks became spirited defenders of the tsars and, as such, were often selected to serve as their bodyguards. As a result, after the revolution of 1917 terminated the tsarist rule, Cossacks were severely persecuted.

14 Most historians consider Alexander III, the Tsar of Russia from 1881 until his death in 1894, a highly conservative ruler. He opposed all liberal reforms and even reversed some of those originated by his more progressive father, Alexander II, including an impending constitution. During Alexander III's reign, Russia fought no major wars, and, as a result, he was nicknamed the "peacemaker." He was a staunch supporter of autocratic rule, the Russian Orthodox Church, nationalism, and, in his spare time, the Russian ballet.

15 In 1861, Alexander II issued the Emancipation Manifesto, eliminating individual serfdom and granting peasants their own land. The decree earned Alexander II the historical role as the "Tsar-Liberator," while in reality the liberated peasants remained poor, with inadequate land, which in turn only deepened their dependence upon the wealthy landlords. To this day, historians debate whether the outcome of the Emancipation Manifesto eventually led to the Russian Revolution of 1917.

16 The emperor's anxiety described by Prince Lev is hardly surprising. Alexander III became the Tsar of Russia after his father, Alexander II, was assassinated by the terrorist group People's Will. As a result, the emperor, in constant fear for his life, was heavily guarded and visited

Saint Petersburg only occasionally. In fact, Saint Petersburg was never safe for members of the royal family. Besides a great number of revolts and revolutions that occurred in the city, three emperors——Peter III, Pavel I, and Alexander II——were assassinated there, as well as heir-to-the-throne Alexei Petrovich, two Ministers of the Interior, and one City Major.

17 Prince Lev's narration of completing the chamber sketch is the most detailed description of *automatism* that I have ever come across. *Automatism* is the involuntary muscular movement in a living person caused by a spirit. Such movement is often manifested in *automatic writing* or *automatic drawing*, during which the spirit takes possession of a person's hand holding a pencil to paper. Persons with psychic abilities regularly employ automatic writing in order to deliver messages from the dead.

18 Olga Lvovna describes a *séance*, a practice fashionable at that time in the homes of the Saint Petersburg's aristocracy. During the séance, a so-called *medium*, a highly sensitive person capable of communicating with the dead, would attempt to engage a specific spirit in a conversation. The participants of the séance, usually men and women wishing to converse with loved ones who have passed away, would be seated around the table, holding hands. After the medium made contact with a spirit, the participants of the séance would question it, and the medium would relay the spirit's answers.

EUGENE YELCHIN

What is your favorite childhood memory?

The communal apartment where Sasha Zaichik lives with his father in *Breaking Stalin's Nose* is similar to the one I grew up in. In addition to my family, several other families had to share one kitchen, one toilet, and one sink with a cold-water tap. My father and mother, my grandmother, and my brother and I were crowded into one small room. At night when the sofas, cots, and folding chairs were converted into beds, the only room left for my small cot was under our round dinner table. On the underside of the tabletop were pencil marks left by the carpenter who built the table.

I couldn't understand their meaning, but one night, I snuck in a pencil and began adding my own scribbles to his. Soon, the bottom of the tabletop was covered with my drawings that no one knew about. For the first time, I felt the power of creating a world that was all my own. This is my favorite childhood memory because I believe that secretly drawing on the underside of that table triggered my future life as an artist.

As a young person, who did you look up to most?

Like most young boys, I was taken with my father. He seemed solid and strong to me then, but looking back now, I'm amazed at what a paradoxical man he actually was. My father was a tough, competitive soccer player who at the same time was fond of Russian poetry and loved to recite it to his teammates! But his main contradiction was this: He understood the oppressive reality of living under Communism, yet he was a devoted Communist. That paradox was lost on me then. As a kid, I didn't know our reality was oppressive; I didn't know of any other. Having a Communist father, I took the Communist ideals for granted. Only later as a teenager did I begin questioning my father's beliefs, which consequently created a rift between us. The disillusionment with my father's

Communist ideals ran parallel to my own maturity. Year after year, I was shedding my father's sway over me while struggling not to lose my love for him.

What was your favorite book when you were a kid?

When I was a kid, good books in Russia were hard to come by because the government controlled the publishing industry. Millions of copies of mediocre propagandistic works were published, while outstanding authors were suppressed. However, there was a series of illustrated books called The Adventure and Science Fiction Library that included classic novels by Jules Verne, Alexandre Dumas, Jack London, Robert Louis Stevenson, and other excellent writers. My parents' friends were able to collect the entire series, and often while visiting with them, I'd lose track of time poring over those precious volumes. Years later, the family who owned the books was able to immigrate to the United States. They settled in Minneapolis, and I flew to see them. Amazingly, they had brought The Adventure and Science Fiction Library along. Pulling those books off the shelf, I realized that over forty years had passed since I'd last opened them. In that distant past, I must have read them very closely and looked at the pictures even closer, because I remembered every single line in the drawings of cowboys, knights, and pirates that I'd loved so much as a child.

What do you consider to be your greatest accomplishment?

What I value most is the ability to make a personal choice in spite of circumstances. Often, it seems impossible to make such a choice because of the outside pressure or fear of repercussions. My greatest accomplishment is the same as that of every immigrant who came to the United States. I dared to leave behind the country of my birth. Compared with so many others, my life in Russia was good at the time. I had a successful artistic career and food on my table. I was and still am proud to be part of a rich Russian culture. Yet, deep inside, I knew that to remain a citizen of the Soviet Union would implicate me in the crimes of my government. I did everything I could to leave Russia. But that is another story.

All Sasha wants is to become a young Soviet
Pioneer . . . until his father is taken.

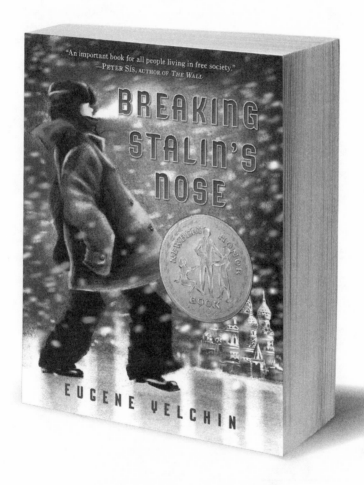

"An important book for all people living in free society."
—PETER SÍS, AUTHOR OF *THE WALL*

BREAKING
STALIN'S
NOSE

NEWBERY HONOR BOOK

EUGENE YELCHIN

Keep reading for a sneak peek!

MY DAD IS A HERO and a Communist and, more than anything, I want to be like him. I can never be like Comrade Stalin, of course. He's our great Leader and Teacher.

The voice on the radio says, "Soviet people, follow our great Leader and Teacher—the beloved Stalin—forward and ever forward to Communism! Stalin is our banner! Stalin is our future! Stalin is our happiness!" Then a song comes on, "A Bright Future Is Open to Us." I know every word, and, singing along, I take out a pencil and paper and start writing.

Dear Comrade Stalin,

I want to thank you personally for my happy childhood. I am fortunate to live in the Soviet Union, the most democratic and progressive country in the world. I have read how hard the lives of children are in the capitalist countries and I feel pity for all those who do not live in the USSR. They will never see their dreams come true.

My greatest dream has always been to join the Young Soviet Pioneers—the most important step in becoming a real Communist like my dad. By the time I was one year old, my dad had taught me the Pioneers greeting. He would say, "Young Pioneer! Ready to fight for the cause of the Communist Party and Comrade Stalin?" In response, I would raise my hand in the Pioneers salute. Of course, I couldn't reply "Always ready!" like the real Pioneers do; I couldn't talk yet. But I'm old enough now and my dream is becoming a reality. Tomorrow at my school's Pioneers rally, I will finally become a Pioneer.

It's not possible to be a true Pioneer without training one's character in the Stalinist spirit.

Дорогой товарищ
Сталин

BREAKING STALIN'S NOSE

I solemnly promise to make myself strong from physical exercise, to forge my Communist character, and always to be vigilant, because our capitalist enemies are never asleep. I will not rest until I am truly useful to my beloved Soviet land and to you personally, dear Comrade Stalin. Thank you for giving me such a wonderful opportunity.

> *Forever yours,*
> *Sasha Zaichik,*
> *Moscow Elementary School #37*

When I imagine Comrade Stalin reading my letter, I get so excited that I can't sit still. I rise up and march like a Pioneer around the room, then head to the kitchen to wait for my dad.